We believe that we live in a perfectly mundane and understandable world, where everything "makes sense" and can be explained by Science and logic and cold, hard facts. It is all as plain, and immutable, and rational as electric lights, and "stimulus–response", and income tax.

But that's not how it really is...

Magick is here with us. Magick lies all around us, concealed from us by our inability or unwillingness to see it. The magickal world lies close next to our world, like two pages in a single book –and when someone turns a page to see what happens next in the story, interesting things can happen...

The Lands
That Lie
Between

An urban fantasy

With Morgan and Sam

The Lands That Lie Between

An urban fantasy
With Morgan and Sam

By Catherine Kane

Foresight Publications
Wallingford, Ct.

The Lands That Lie Between ©Aug2012
by Catherine Kane

ISBN 978-0-9846951-0-2

Foresight Publications
Wallingford, CT,

To my father,

Raymond L. Shoup,

who first introduced me
to fantasy
and the power of story
and who has
always
been my hero.

This one's for you, Dad

Acknowledgements

There's one name on the cover, but it takes more folks than that to make a book happen. And here come some of them now.

To Jayee WhiteOak for proofreading, feedback and commentary at lightning speed under very unreasonable circumstances. Despite it not being your genre, you gave me just the feedback I needed.

To Morgan, for letting me run off with your name when catastrophe threatened.

To the members of the Fairfield County Writer's group and their fearless leader, CJ, for encouragement and inspiration and support and kindness online and in person. A writer needs a tribe.

To my friends who gave me permission to borrow your appearances and mannerisms to base characters on. (No, they're not you, but they may feel familiar.) You know who you are- and if not, please have fun looking...

To my family, who've encouraged my writing since I was very small (and still do, now that I've graduated to fun sized.)

And most of all, to my husband Sean, whose love, patience, and support makes my writing possible. You are the start of every adventure.

Table of Contents

Prelude

The doctor stood by the bedside of the dying summer king in the darkened room.

Bending, he listened to the labored breathing, and then took his patient's wrist to feel for the soft and thready pulse. The summer king's heart was slowing, slowing, moving towards the end of life; and all that meant for the faerie court, both seelie and unseelie.

He held the cup to the parched and cracking lips, coaxing a tiny sip of tonic into his patient's mouth. The herbs and liquid would make the summer king more comfortable, but there was nothing more to be done to hold back the inevitable.

And this was a death that would mean great changes, not only for the dying summer king and his relations, but also for all of the inhabitants of the Lands that Lie Between.

Straightening, he gestured to the nurse to continue to keep her watch upon the king; to do what she could to keep him comfortable and safe.

The doctor left the room. Outside in the corridor, the steward stood silent, awaiting his diagnosis of the king's condition.

"What word, then?" he asked. "Will the summer king rally and return to us once more?"

"I fear not." The doctor told him. "I've done all that I can do, and, at this point, it is only a question of keeping him comfortable as he passes to the lands Beyond these."

"Are you sure?" the steward pleaded. "Is there no other healer, no other remedy that might restore him to his health and vigor? "

The doctor sighed. "I was chosen as royal physician these many years ago, because in all the land, my healing skills were judged to surpass all others. I've spent my life learning further skills to be the best healer possible; and forming connections with other healers, to further strengthen the knowledge at my command. I've given my years to being familiar with the health needs of the royal family, and adjusting my treatments to suit each noble scion."

"And if there's some cure that would serve, I know not of it."

"I fear that the summer king will die. And very soon."

The steward raised his head, a look of determination on his honest face.

"Then the call must be sounded." He said.

"The court must be summoned."

"And all must be prepared for the transition of power in the Lands that Lie Between."

The doctor nodded, a troubled look on his face.

One
Morgan

The day that Morgan lost her job, she broke her lease, threw everything that she valued in life (including her cat, Sam) into her van, kissed her adoptive parents and her little brother good bye and started on a cross-country trek.

Morgan had wanderlust. She'd felt for a very long time as if she was marking time. . .waiting. . .

Waiting for what she couldn't say. It felt as if her life had been spent on hold, listening to cosmic muzak, waiting for the operator of Fate to pick up and connect her to her Destiny.

Whatsoever that might be.

So when her job went away, and she found herself with no romantic connection, no close friends, no job and no expectations (other than waiting for that Operator), it seemed like a sign.

A sign of what, she wasn't sure, but a sign nonetheless; and when you've got a guiding light, you've got to follow that star.

This wasn't like her. Morgan was usually more cautious. When she encountered something new, she liked to kick the tires, take it for a test drive, ask three associates what they thought of it, Google it online, and so on.

But an invisible wind was blowing through her world, and she felt the need to leave, go, travel the globe, have adventures, meet exotic people, try food she'd never tasted, see horizons she'd never seen.

So she took to the road.

Many months later, here she was in a new home in a new town, hip deep in boxes and clutter and possibilities. She'd found a funky second floor walk up, with oddly shaped rooms and stained glass windows and a flavor all its own, in a distinctive old building full of eccentricities. She was now standing in the middle of it, trying to figure out the best way to pull everything together and make it truly her own. She'd set up her computer, and found places for her reading chair, bed and bookcases; and Sam was gleefully engaged in turning loose packing materials into sporting equipment, and making every other place his own, so all of the most important stuff was done. There were still an awful lot of boxes still awaiting sorting and distributing, though.

The next box in the pile was full of coffee mugs and potholders. "I could start bailing this stuff into the kitchen, and organize it later," she thought. "That would clear a bunch of boxes, and I'll need those things to cook and eat at home. Eating here will stretch the budget until I can find work."

She took the box and picked her way across the crowded living room, only to stop dead when she reached the kitchen arch. Her dish towels were hanging on the dish rack.

"I don't remember doing that," she thought confusedly. "Of course, I've been doing so much and working so hard that it's possible I just picked them up, walked in and hung them up on automatic pilot. Given the amount of dust and clutter I've gone through, having what I need to wash my hands and face available would be a great thought."

4

"After all, I've been in here all day and no one else has been in this apartment. Except for Sam, of course. But, last that I knew, he pulls things out, not puts them away"

"Sam!" she shouted. "Did you hang up the kitchen towels? "

The wiry golden tabby cat gave her a look, and then ever so c-a-s -u–a–l–l–y started cleaning himself. He was very clearly too innocent a cat to be messing about with such radical things as dish towels.

"Not you, then" she grinned. "Then I must just be more ruthlessly efficient than I thought."

"Or else, be losing my mind; but hey, with all this unpacking, I'm entitled!" she laughed, the odd moment past and put aside.

The Lands That Lie Between

Two
Morgan

The following day, after a hard day of job hunting, Morgan was walking down a side street near her apartment. To reward herself for looking for work, she decided to stop in at Mystic Miscellanea, the local fun and funky temple of used books, health food, new age supplies, and other eclectic delights.

Once in, the fresh herbs, gently used novels, and soothing music drew her deeper into the store.

She waved at the store owner. "What's new?" she asked.

"We've starting having readers in on Tuesdays" the owner replied. "We've got an excellent tarot reader here today. Ever had your cards read?"

"No, never," said Morgan honestly "but I've always wanted to."

The other woman grinned. "Great. This fellow is the right one to start with. Can I interest you in a quick dance with the cards?"

"Why not?" thought Morgan. "I've been curious about this kind of thing, and someone with this kind of recommendation sounds like the right person to see."

"Sign me up!" she said.

The woman smiled and turned to pull back a curtain at the back of the store, revealing a small and cozy private area. In the niche, a bearded man with flowing silver hairs and a mass of esoteric necklaces sat behind a tiny table. He looked at her kindly and gestured, inviting her to sit down.

"Never had a tarot reading before?" he said. "Well,

let me explain a few things first"

"First, you need to know about free will. You have it, and that means you can make choices and, by doing that, change the direction of your life and affect its quality. Make better choices, you increase the odds of having a better life, right?"

Morgan nodded.

"Well, any good reading is going to tell you what happens if you keep doing things the way you've been doing them. Don't like something in a reading? Then you need to change what you're doing to change where you're headed. Any negative cards should be seen as warnings of things you can now avoid because you know about them."

"In other words, the future is engraved, not so much in stone as in really, really cold cream cheese."

"Is that how this works?" said Morgan.

"Yes." he smiled. "I'm kind of like the traffic guy on the road of life. I'm here to tell you where the traffic jams are, so you can take an alternate route if you like. Now, do you have a specific question or do you just want a general reading?"

She thought for a moment.

"I'm not sure," she said nervously. "I've been feeling for a long time like my life was on hold, like I was waiting for something. When I lost my job earlier this year, that waiting feeling led to me packing up and traveling cross country, finally ending up here. I'd really like some insight into that. Can the cards tell me about something like that? "

"They sure can." he smiled. "Let's see what they have to say." He reached into a pouch and pulled out a well-worn, well-loved pack of cards. Looking carefully at her, he shuffled them, and had her cut them.

"And now, we begin." he said.

He dealt out several cards in a pattern on the table and looked at them for a moment.

"This card is you and new beginnings," he began "and this second card sees you going on a journey. No, wait; make that more of a quest, for there is a goal to be accomplished and obstacles to be overcome. A mystery from out of your past will arise and change everything you know, sending you into movement."

He drew three more cards and laid out each in turn.

"There will be challenges," he said seriously. "There will be those who oppose you. There will be danger; but there will also be surprising allies and help from unexpected places. You will walk alone in darkness before emerging into the light."

Three cards more joined their fellows.

"To succeed, you must do three things. You must face your fear. You must trust the wisdom within you. And you must help those who have less than you do without any thought of yourself."

A final card was played above the others.

"And in the end," he said "whether you succeed or fail depends on the choices you've made. This is a case where doing the right thing, even in the little things that don't seem to matter, may have great repercussions."

The reader looked up at her thoughtfully. "Now is there anything here that you need explained?"

She sat back, her head whirling from what she had just heard.

"I'm not quite sure," she said finally. "There's an awful lot of stuff here, and I'm still trying to take it all in. It sounds like some dramatic fantasy story, with magic and heroes and peril dire."

He smiled. "There's actually more magick afoot in the everyday world than most people realize. That's because most people tune it out. Most people have all they can do to deal with unemployment and taxes and what thing is unhealthy to eat this week, without actually taking in the fact that magick works, that creatures from fantasy are often based in fact, and that the world is really a more enchanted place than they understand. It is easier to deal with these things by tuning them out, by not seeing things you don't want to believe in. "

"But that doesn't mean the magick isn't there," he added. "It just slips between the layers of their awareness, like a book mark between two pages. And when the magickal world makes things happen noticeably, most people will explain it away. They'll come up with a "rational explanation" which is really a kind of fairy story about how what really happened couldn't possibly have happened."

"It's just some of us who see both sides-bright and dark, sun and moon, mundanity and magick. And when you walk with one foot in each land, you get a feel for a world that's bigger than most people believe."

"So, yes, it looks like you've been waiting for a quest that's on its way. Most of us are on some kind of quest or another. It just looks like yours is going to be a bit more dramatic and magical than the average one."

"Magical?" she said. "Like elves and talking animals and alakazam?"

He laughed at her startled expression. "Exactly like elves and talking animals and alakazam!" he said. "Magick is all around you. There's magick in the power of prayer, and the body's ability to heal itself. There's magick in the power of positive thinking, and how thoughts become things. There's magick in creativity, and love, and the impossible things that people are doing every day. Magick is the glue that holds the Universe together, and knowing this is so gives you the ability to change what's to what could be."

Everything he was saying was far from anything she'd ever experienced, but still it somehow rang true.

She seized on one part of what he was saying. "Elves, you said. You mean there are really elves?"

"Yes," he replied more seriously "but they don't always like being referred to by that particular name. They're more properly called the Sidhe, the Fae or, to be respectful, the Gentry, the Good Folk or the Fair Folk. Not a bad thing to be respectful, too. You never know who might be listening."

"Little tinkly winged people elves?' she asked in disbelief.

"No." he said seriously. "What you're thinking of are Victorian constructs, pretty tales created to amuse children. What I'm speaking of are the Good Folk, who come from much further back in time, and are full-sized beings, but different from humans. Many of them are beautiful and terrible and powerful beyond measure. Many others walk in seemings that are strange to our eyes. The sidhe are divided into two courts, one of the Light and one of the Darkness, called seelie and unseelie, but even the seelie sidhe, who are in theory good, can still be dangerous to humans around them. They're not like us, and it is well to remember that."

She stared at him, dumbfounded. "You're saying elves are walking the streets of modern America?" she said. "How can that be? Why don't we hear about them?"

"I'm saying that the sidhe, both seelie and unseelie, are inhabitants of this country, just as you and I are. They walk the streets that lie Between our streets. Their homes are hidden Between our homes. They walk in powerful disguises. They haunt the shadows and the night, and walk at noon as well, cloaked by our expectations."

"They're more powerful than us individually, but there are far more of us than there are of them. Because of this, they may look down on us, but they're also careful to avoid drawing attention to themselves. Because a single sidhe may have power over a single mortal human, but en masse, there are more than enough of us to be a threat to their green and pleasant lands."

"And so they shelter in the Between places, where mortal eyes do not go. At crossroads, on staircases, in doorways, in all the places that are neither one thing nor the other. In the Lands that Lie Between. And when they chose to walk abroad, they mask themselves with glamourye, hide themselves in shadows, or disguise themselves with the ability of the human mind to refuse to see what it chooses not to."

"You don't hear about them because, as long as they don't act in ways that betray their uncanny nature, people don't want to hear about them. For most people, it's safer to believe in a non-magickal world, and so they do; and since the sidhe don't fit in such a world, we edit out all notice of their presence, as long as they take care not to betray themselves."

He looked at her, troubled.

"I've been feeling for some time that things are building up, and others in the psychic community have been feeling similar reverberations. When unquiet energy is in motion, it comes many times from some uncanny source, and increasing activity in the sidhe courts is certainly one possible explanation."

"Given the unsettled nature of the energy, the feedback I'm getting from my own intuition and the intuitive community and the likelihood of Fae involvement, I'm not seeing your arrival in this city as co-incidence. The information we have just gotten from the tarot cards only supports this."

He looked kindly at her. "I'm sorry. That's a lot of information to take in, especially for your first reading. I'll bet you need some time to think about all of this."

She nodded. "Do you really believe that this "waiting" feeling means something big is ahead of me?"

"I'm afraid so. The cards say that something almost mythic is coming soon in your life. It is my job to give you a heads up so you can prepare."

Reaching down, he pulled out a business card and passed it to her. "I'm getting the impression that your waiting is almost over with, and that things are going to start moving extremely fast for you. You may find that you need some more advice or even something more than that."

"If you want to learn more about the sidhe, and other information like that, there's a lot of information on our website that might be of use to you. If you've got questions, you can reach myself or my wife at the phone number or e-mail on the card, or check our website for places to find us in person. "

"If you need help, you can also call on us. We know a thing or two about this sort of thing, and we've got connections with other people who do as well. If you need help or advice, don't feel shy about asking."

Taking the card, she got up from the table, her head spinning. "Thank you." she said, tucking the card away for future reference.

Deep in thought, she left Mystic Miscellanea.

She didn't notice the figures that followed her on her way home.

Three
Elsewhere

The first Call to the court had gone out when the summer king had fallen ill...

The second Call to the court had gone out when it became clear to all that the summer king would not recover...

And, soon, very soon, the third and final Call would be sounded...

The Lands That Lie Between

Four
Morgan

And things kept happening around Morgan.

Odd things.

Boxes emptied and tidily stacked. Her bed made. A load of dishes washed and left carefully in the drainer.

Things she didn't remember doing.

And, as for her computer...

She'd come home from a hard day of job hunting and find the computer up and running. Find it open on sites on subjects she'd never even thought about.

Like historic beliefs about faeries and other supernatural beings; different ways of tapping into your intuition; and dream interpretation.

When she checked the computer's history, she found other sites she was sure she'd never looked at. Like ones tracking recent crime statistics; exploring local folklore; and relating fictional stories of machinations and plots of an imaginary court in an imaginary world.

Morgan found herself becoming paranoid.

She inspected the locks for signs of being picked or forced. She found none.

She interrogated the landlord, who held the only other known key to her apartment. He assured her that he had not gone into her apartment, nor did he want to. She asked about prior tenants who might have kept a key. The landlord assured her that locks were changed between each tenant to prevent any problems.

She found she believed him.

She tapped into spy literature, lifting ways to mark

her home against invasion. She tried a hair on the door frame, a pile of jangly things behind a door, a string trap draped in concealment across a window frame, to try to find out how the mysterious housekeeper was getting in.

All in vain. None of her traps or tricks stopped her tidy visitor, or even told her how he was getting in.

She even caught herself looking suspiciously at Sam, her cat. Only for a moment, but still…

"I must be walking in my sleep," she thought. "But that doesn't explain things that happen when I'm out."

"There's too much unexplained to be chalked up to forgetfulness. There's something going on here, but I'm damned if I can figure out what it is."

And later that night, she found out…

Five
Elsewhere

The steward was troubled, and he was unsure why.

For as long as he could remember, the health of the land, both the Lands Between and the human lands, had been linked with the fortunes of the King.

When the king was noble and honorable, a seelie or summer king, the Light flourished and all was well. Crops grew in abundance, weather was seasonable and mild, and people of all types were tolerant, compassionate and kind to each other.

When, on the other hand, an unseelie king ruled and winter was in the hearts of his subjects, famine and flood and intolerance were the harvest.

And, since the Lands Between and the human lands were mirrors of each other, drawing energy from each other, the fate of the human lands was shaped by who ruled the Lands Between.

The present king was a summer king, a kind and honorable seelie monarch, and his reign had been long and prosperous, but, as he failed, so did the lands both human and Lands Between.

And when he died, who would reign next would determine the fate of both worlds.

As the fae kings died, the power and majesty that they held was gradually released, slipping out into the world and lodging in their heirs. The calling would go out, calling all possessing even a touch of that spark to return to court, that the next ruler be chosen with all in attendance.

And when the king would die, the next ruler would

be determined by how much of that power had returned to court.

Light or darkness/seelie or unseelie/kindly summer or cruel winter sovereign-whichever side had called home the most power would reign.

The steward shook his head. This was a system that had served the worlds well for as long as he could remember, yet now he had an uneasy feeling that told him something was not right.

Reaching the top of the tower, he shook his head and reached for the rope. Bracing himself, he pulled vigorously and the brazen Bell of Ages sounded out.

And the Call went out to all the heirs…

Six
Morgan

She'd been dreaming – dreaming a powerful dream. One of those dreams where you feel like you're awake.

In her dream, she heard a horn sound, and the sound of the horn caught at her, drawing her to find it. Over mountain and undersea she passed, through fire and shadow and ice, ever following the call of the horn.

There were other figures there, misty and indistinct. Some also drawn by the call of the horn. Some rose up before her, sword on hand, and tried to bar her way.

She saw a castle draped in black. She saw a dying king and a dying land. And she heard a voice cry out "A door closes, and the road opens. The traveler must be quick, before the Darkness closes it…"

And she woke, blinking her eyes and wondering which world was the dreaming one and which was the waking…

"That was a bit pretentious." she thought fuzzily after a moment. And then a noise in the kitchen brought her bolt awake, her breath catching in her throat.

Slowly, stealthily, she slipped from the bed. Taking a bedside lamp in her hand as the best weapon available, Morgan crept quietly to the kitchen arch. She peered in, and saw something extremely odd…

In the moonlight streaming through the kitchen, Morgan could not at first spot the source of the noise. When she squinted, however, the scene pulled into focus and she saw the little men.

Little men. No taller than a hand's length.

Little men in homespun clothing hanging up her dish towels, wiping down the kitchen counter, sweeping up the floor with the crumb broom.

Little men, working in tandem, washing and drying her dishes, and loading them into the cabinets.

Impossibly little men.

Morgan's mouth gaped wide open. The lamp dropped from her hand, clattering against the floor.

As one, a hundred little heads snapped around. Two hundred little eyes fixed on her. And in a heartbeat, the kitchen was empty, save only for the light of the moon.

"Brownies," said a voice behind her. "They don't like people watching them work, so they're outa here until the next time they can creep back again when no one's looking to do some more housework."

Just like the brownies, her head snapped around at the unexpected noise, heart in mouth. She snatched up the lamp to defend herself against the intruder…

But the only face in sight was Sam, her cat.

Cats don't talk. There must be someone else hiding here. She looked quickly from side to side, searching frantically for the source of the voice.

"Down here" came a sardonic yet friendly voice.

She looked down.

"Right down here." her cat said "Yes, it's me, talking to you."

She stared at him wide eyed.

Sam sighed. He'd often seemed exasperated with the foolishness of humans.

"Yes, you're awake, Morgan. It's me, your cat, talking to you." he said again.

Morgan fainted.

She awoke to the sensation of a soft paw, gently patting at her face.

"Morgan, honey, wake up. I'm sorry to spring this on you so suddenly, but things are happening in the Lands Between. Things are happening fast, and I need to bring you up to speed even faster so you can do what you need to do in the days to come."

"Come on, Morgan. Come back to the land of the living here."

She opened her eyes to a worried golden furry face, golden eyes looking deeply into hers.

"Morgan? No time for cat naps now. There's a lot I need to tell you, and not much time left. I need you to wake up, sit up, and focus, girlfriend. Then I need you to stand up, go to the fridge and get out that left over prime rib and give it to the nice kitty. . ."

"Hey!" said Morgan sitting up and staring at the tabby. "That's my lunch!"

"Just checking if you were paying attention," said the cat, grinning ever so slightly. "But now we do have some things to talk about, and we need to talk fast."

The Lands That Lie Between

Seven
Elsewhere

There were hunters in the night.

A pale, slight figure came out of the bodega with an armful of bags to the cheerful jangle of the bells on the door. The healer had finally found the herbs she needed for the healing work she practiced at the homeless shelter, and she was feeling happy. She walked purposefully down the street towards the bus stop three blocks away.

A furry form on four legs slunk out of the alley, vaguely snarling under its breath. Another followed it. Then, a third. All following her

The shopper froze slightly, then continued to walk faster. Behind her, the pack crept forward, increasing its speed.

With a shout, she threw her bags behind her and broke into a run for the bus stop. There'd be people there, and her pursuers wouldn't be able to do anything so obvious.

The pack bayed and leapt in pursuit.

Panting, the shopper ran full tilt-almost to the bus stop. "There's someone there!" she thought."Safe haven!"

Then the person waiting for the bus turned and looked at her. And stood up. And up. And up.

And her hopes died.

And, shortly after, she did, too.

The Lands That Lie Between

Eight
Morgan

"…And that's why you've been feeling like you've been waiting for so long," said Sam. "You have. You have elven blood from your ancestors. You're one of those the power devolves to, as the old King passes."

It had been a few hours since they started talking, and Morgan was still having a hard time with all of this. "Power?" she said. "Like super powers? Do I get x-ray vision or super strength or fabulous magical abilities or something like that?"

Sam made as disgusted a face as he could with his bone structure. "No, not super powers, you nit" he said. "This isn't a comic book. It's more like some kind of elven tontine. When the present king dies, his power redistributes itself amongst all possible heirs, who are supposed to trot their butts back to court on the double when the Call goes out, in order to see fair play in who reigns next."

"Whichever faction is supported by the majority of power present is the one who puts their guy on the throne next. And whosoever reigns determines what kind of world it is, both for the human world and for the Lands Between. You see, the nature of the land is linked to the nature of the king, and the nature of the human world is linked to the nature of the Lands Between. We're all connected."

"You don't do card tricks with this kind of power. You bring it back to court as your price of admission, and as your qualification to back a candidate of your choice. Now do you get it?"

"Well, I think it's ridiculous" said Morgan. "Why

do we have to drop everything and run over there? Why can't I just phone in my vote?"

"Because it's not a flipping vote!" exploded Sam. "It's a contribution to a side. And because they're elves, and this is how elves have done this for millions of years! And because elves don't use cell phones! Now do you get it?"

"It still seems way out there to me…" said Morgan. "And speaking of way out there, how long have you been a talking cat, anyway? A talking cat? Who has a talking cat? And why do I have a talking cat, anyway?"

Sam looked a bit abashed for a minute.

"As the present king has ebbed, odd things have been happening in the court. Little things by themselves, but weaving a bigger pattern of something not right. When you were born, certain people thought it best to hide you to keep you safe from any harm. You were placed with a nice couple, who didn't know your somewhat colorful heritage, and I was set to watch over you and keep you safe."

"I'd wondered how you managed to live that long and still be in such great shape." Morgan said.

Sam preened. "Thanks" he said. "I work out."

"But why are you only talking now?" she asked.

"Up to now," he said "there was nothing to say."

She gave him a look. He looked back at her innocently, with a facial expression that said "No, I didn't eat the canary."

"No, really" he rushed, seeing a load of steam build up between her ears. "There was always the chance that nothing would happen-that the summer king would live beyond your mortal years and that you'd never have to take action at all in the Lands that Lie Between."

"That's another thing." She said. "The Lands that Lie Between? What kind of a crazy name is that for a place? "

"What kind of a name is Kensington, for that matter?" asked the cat irritably "…but we live here."

"The Lands that Lie Between is a pretty good name, actually," he continued. "The entrances to elven lands have always been found in the in-between spaces-places that are neither one place or another. Crossroads. Stairs. Hallways. Doorways. Shared walls. And all of the other spots that are neither fish nor fowl nor good red meat. That's where to find the entrance to enchantment, and that's also where you're most likely to spy one of the Good Folk coming or going to the mortal world. That's why they call them the Lands Between."

"Getting back to why I'm talking now–it's because things are coming to a head now. The summer king is dying, and his time is almost gone. His power is slipping gradually away to his heirs in worlds both mystical and mundane. And the Call has gone out, for all those who bear that power to return to the court."

"You heard the Call too. Didn't you ever wonder what possessed you to move cross country at the drop of a hat?"

Morgan was silent. It'd seemed so logical at the time, but, now that she thought on it, it did seem most odd and unlike her.

"And furthermore, we're going to have to leave soon and move quickly" said the cat. "There are rumors that some of the heirs have disappeared. It seems like the

Unseelie court is making a major grab for control."

"I've managed to keep you under wraps so far, but it's only a matter of time before the Forces of Darkness home in on you here, so you and I have got to hit the road pronto. This apartment hasn't been a permanent residence for many years. That means that the protection of its hearth is rather limited, and I would just as soon be elsewhere if the unseelie sidhe come knocking."

Morgan felt her head spinning. Fantasy as reality? The Lands Between? The Forces of Darkness? Unseelie sidhe? Power inside of her? Elven courts? Calling to Return? This was all more than she could take in at once.

"So, I'm one of the heirs to an elven king?" she blurted out. "Does that mean that I'm a fairy princess?"

Sam turned and froze her with the look of mingled fondness and contempt for human idiocy that cats excel at.

"No, your Highness" he said sarcastically. "You're not anything close to a flipping *Fairy Princess. . ."*

"You're a very small player in a very big game, with high stakes. You're a very small player, but still important, because the power you carry may be enough to decide whether Light or Darkness rules both this world and the Lands Between. You're a woman at serious risk of injury or death, because there are players in this game that don't play fairly. You're the owner of a wise, magnificent cat, who'd just as soon keep his beautiful hide intact, thank you, and who thinks you ought to be much more concerned with that concept. And finally, you're someone who really ought to get her butt in gear, if she wants to be out when the Bad Guys come calling."

"But, certainly not a flipping Fairy Princess" he

said. "My blood sugar levels will simply not permit it."

"What? I still don't understand. . ." said Morgan.

The cat started to reply, and then froze. His head turned and he seemed to listen to something in the distance for a moment.

"We don't have time for you to understand right now" Sam said cautiously after a moment. "It's time to move. I'll have to explain the rest of it to you as we go along, but we need to start moving now."

"Now, get your butt moving and grab what you'll need to be all right while we get mobile and stay mobile. Money. Checks and credit cards too, though it's better not to use them as they're traceable. Car keys. Warm clothing, in layers, including things that you can use to disguise yourself or conceal your appearance. Toothbrush and hairbrush. Snacks, including lots of food for the nice kitty."

The cat loped across the living room and leapt to the windowsill, pawing aside the curtains and looking out.

Still confused by all she'd heard, but struck by the tone of increasing urgency in the golden cat's voice, Morgan got up and went into the bedroom. Reaching into her closet, she pulled out a duffle bag with a shoulder strap and began to fill it with things Sam had listed.

She paused for a moment, with bag half full, debating the merits of cardigan versus sweat shirt. Sam poked his head around the door frame and stared at her, tail lashing slightly.

"No time for fashion choices," he hissed. "We need to get a move on!"

This was not the first time that Morgan had been bullied by her cat, but it was certainly the oddest one. Her head still spinning, she scrambled to grab a few more things from the bathroom and jam them into the duffle bag and her over sized purse.

She grabbed up the duffle bag by the shoulder strap, slung her purse over one shoulder, threw on an oversized coat, and grabbed the car keys. Sam was already at the door, pawing vigorously at it in his eagerness to be gone.

Then suddenly, Sam froze again, body stiff, tail out straight, ears erect in the intent listening position that she knew so well. He cocked his head to listen and then sniffed cautiously, and sniffed once more.

"Morgan, honey, we may be running just a little bit later than I'd hoped for here, "he said very quietly. "I want you to move very, very quietly over here to me, and open the door just a smidge, but don't stick your head out or try to go out the door. Make as little noise as you can- we don't want to alert anything. Most of all, don't panic. Leave the hard work up to me."

Her heart suddenly in her mouth, Morgan ghosted across the floor. She put her hand of the door knob and turned it slowly, silently, breathing a prayer that the hinges wouldn't creak for once. She pulled the door open a couple of inches, and peered out above as Sam did below.

The hallway seemed much darker than it had when she'd come home earlier in the day, and unwelcoming in a way it never had before. It was absolutely silent, but the silence of those times when things are just about to happen, and Nature holds its breath and waits. Morgan's skin crawled just looking out, and she couldn't face the thought of actually going out there.

And then she heard noises in the stairwell at the

other end of the hall-footsteps, multiple footsteps coming up the stairs, getting closer and closer...

A paw on her knee almost made her shriek. Catching herself in time, Morgan looked down and saw Sam's looking up at her. He nodded, and pawed the back of the door, signaling her to close it again.

Morgan eased the door closed, double locked it, and then let out the breath that she hadn't realized she was holding until that moment.

"Too late, way too late" muttered Sam frantically. "And if they're coming up the front staircase, they've probably got someone watching the fire escapes too. We need to get out, but how to do it?"

A quiet knock came at the door. They both froze in place for a moment.

"What about the garbage lift?" hissed Morgan, also frantic. "Would that work? Is it big enough?"

Sam's head snapped up. "Could be-let's see, shall we?" he cried, as they both dashed for the kitchen.

One of the more questionable amenities of this antique apartment was a dumbwaiter, leftover from the apartment's days as a flat in a bijou luxury residence. Long ago, it had been used to send up gourmet dinners to the town house residents, and send garbage to the basement to be disposed of. When the luxury flats decayed, and were converted into low-income apartments, the dumbwaiters were left in place but pad locked for security's sake.

Could they open it in time? Was the dumbwaiter still in the shaft? Would it hold one woman and one very handsome cat? Could they get it to move? Would it support them or would they plummet to their doom? Many questions, but time was short, and only action would give them their answers.

The knock came again, slightly louder now.

Morgan shuddered as she fumbled with the lock on the dumbwaiter cover. The tarot reader had told her to trust her instincts, and her instincts told her anything was better than facing that corridor and what was out there in it now.

The lock was stuck from years of disuse. Morgan drew a deep breath and managed to force it open, despite its own personal inclinations. She pulled at the dumbwaiter sliding door, also set in its ways and disinclined to movement. By sheer muscle and force of will, she pried it open, making far more noise than she liked in the process.

Sam said "Give me a moment. I'll check it out." and slipped through the half way open sliding door to the dumbwaiter.

The knocking at the door was a pounding now.

Morgan heard her next door neighbor, easily irritated by excess noise, jump to his feet and go storming to his own door, flinging it open.

"What's going on out here?" she heard him shout.

And then he screamed, a scream that sliced into her very soul.

"No" thought Morgan "oh, no…" as she thrust her duffle after Sam through the half open door into the dumbwaiter, and wiggled her way in after it.

There was a silence at the door for a moment, and then the pounding resumed-great, booming blows that made the entire apartment echo.

All of the way into the lift, Morgan wrenched at the inside of the door of the dumbwaiter and forced it closed, and then sat silently hiding in the darkness.

"It's a good thing that cats can see in the dark" said Sam. "It's also a good thing that the lift was still here in the shaft. Morgan, honey, put your hands on the rope here and pull." She felt him nuzzle her hands into position.

"One rope goes up and the other down. We want down. Now's the time to get pulling, because I don't think that door is going to hold out much longer. . ."

As Sam finished speaking, they heard the front door shatter, with pieces flying violently in all directions. Morgan squeaked and began to pull furiously on the rope. Fortunately, the first rope she touched was the one that started them downwards.

They heard heavy footsteps rush into the apartment, as Morgan pulled with increased motivation. The dumbwaiter began to move.

The dumbwaiter moved agonizingly slowly despite Morgan's best efforts, groaning and complaining as they inched their way downwards. Above their heads, Morgan and Sam could hear crashing noises, as their apartment was violently searched and then torn apart in frustration and spite. As she pulled, Morgan wept for all of her belongings that were being destroyed, but was glad of the ruckus that masked the noise of their exit. She was also glad that the ropes on the dumbwaiter still seemed strong enough to support their weight, and that the bottom had not fallen out of the dumbwaiter yet.

A seeming eternity later, they touched down at the bottom of the shaft in the basement. Prying open this door proved more challenging. Morgan finally had to lie back and kick through the sliding door. A heap of garbage and a fine assortment of furniture found at the curbside were piled up around the exit, making walking challenging.

"Think you made enough noise?" snarled Sam.

"Since the alternative was sitting in pitch dark in a dumbwaiter until someone found us, I don't see that I had much choice about it." Morgan snapped back at him.

Then, remembering their situation, they grinned sheepishly, leaned into each other for a moment and fell silent again.

Above their heads, they could hear the sound of many large bodies coming down the stairs from their apartment.

"Let's make like a tree and leaf," said Sam. Morgan nodded.

And like that, they were gone.

Into the darkness.

Nine
Elsewhere

Around the corner of the building, a small figure crept cautiously on four legs. The summer king was dying and the court was calling-calling to all who held the escaping power, whether seelie or unseelie, calling them to return to the source, bearing that power with them.

Those who returned would determine who would next rule both the human world and the Lands Between.

Light or Darkness. A delicate balance at the best of times; and the word in the wind was unseelie creatures were arriving, but the seelie ones were going missing at this crucial time.

He was seelie. He was also very small and very afraid. And he was alone. He had tried to contact companions for the journey, but no one had answered.

Somehow, that made him even more afraid.

Cautiously, silently, he slipped through shadows, trying to avoid attention, to stay safe. With every sound he heard, he froze, eyes and ears frantically straining for any sign of danger.

But eyes and ears were not enough to spot the wispy, translucent figure that rose up through the pavement. Stealth and cunning did not serve when the long and bony fingers closed tightly on his throat, dragging him back into the concrete.

Soon, the street was empty.

The Lands That Lie Between

Ten
Morgan

Sam and Morgan ran frantically from the apartment basement, the violent uproar they heard fading behind them lending wings to their feet. Soon the sounds of wholesale destruction had faded, and they ducked into a darkened alley way to take stock and plan their next move.

"I thought you said that the Good Folk preferred to go unnoticed amongst humans!" cried Morgan, breathing heavily. "So what the heck was that all about? They broke through the door! They trashed my apartment! We had to run for our lives! And what about poor Mr. Robinson?! I know he was a bit of a pill, but don't they think someone won't notice that they ate him alive?!?"

"Think about it, Morgan" said Sam, also panting from their headlong flight. "How many home invasions do you hear of in a week? How many break-ins are never solved? As for Mr. Robinson, how many people disappear every year and are never ever heard from again? It's not like he's going to get a chance to tell on them!"

With a sinking heart, Morgan realized what he was saying was true. This put a different slant on how she saw the world around her.

"I'm sorry for Mr. Robinson" said Sam, his voice softening "but I'm also glad that it wasn't us instead. And if we hadn't moved quickly, make no mistake, it would have been. The bottom line here is that, while most of the Fae try to conceal their world's existence, some of them act suddenly and violently, if it serves their needs and if they can do it without exposing their world. Understand this

39

better now?"

Morgan nodded, struck dumb.

"That's good." said Sam. "Now, I don't think that we should hover here for very long. By now, they'll have discovered the trick we played on them, and will be working in circles outwards, trying to catch up with us; but we do have a few minutes in which to figure out where we want to go next."

"Speaking of tricks," he said "the dumbwaiter was a brilliant inspiration. Good thinking, Morgan baby."

Morgan felt herself blush a bit in the darkness. "Thanks" she said. "I owe it all to panic. I definitely didn't want to go out in that hall, and I guess that my instincts were right on that one."

"No, no. . ." Sam said. "That was definitely epic story heroine thinking if I've ever seen it. If you keep that up, I can just lie back and be your attractive sidekick for the rest of this adventure. . ."

Morgan snorted. "Nope, I'm sorry" she said "You'll have to have more than just charm and good looks to pull your weight in this team."

"All right then" he said. "Now, did you lose anything while we were running for our lives? "

"I've got my purse and my duffle, but I'm afraid I lost my keys while leaping in and out of dumbwaiters" she admitted, crestfallen. She adjusted the slide on the shoulder strap of her purse and clipped it around her waist.

"I don't think you'll miss the key to your apartment." said Sam. "I believe the door it fits is no longer in existence. But we will miss your car keys. As a point of interest, you wouldn't happen to know how to hot wire a car?"

"Sorry" said Morgan. "I'm afraid that wasn't on the curriculum when I was at school."

"Drat!" said Sam. "I guess its public transport and shank's mare for us."

"Shank's mare? What's that?" she asked.

"On foot" he said "or carried in the gentle arms of one's loving owner."

"Oh, right then," she said sardonically, bending over to pick him up."

"Now the gates to the eleven court are only open at certain times and they move from place to place" he said as she began to walk.

She stopped dead and looked at him.

"This is another one of those dumb eleven things, right?" she said. "One of those things that makes this so much harder than it has to be?"

He gave her a hard look.

"It's worked for them for millions of years." He said with dignity. "Now the closest gate to the court of the Lands Between opens tomorrow at noon, and remains open until midnight, so we'll need a place to hide out until the ways Between are open. Where can we hole up until then?"

"Well the library's open until ten p.m. tonight," said Morgan "and we can hide out in the stacks overnight. They don't check the building too carefully before they close."

"Right oh!" said Sam "the library, it is then! "

And they set off in that direction.

The Lands That Lie Between

Eleven
Morgan

It was late, but it was amazing how many people were still riding the bus to the heart of the city at this hour. In a certain way, Morgan was glad of that. After all, whatever was chasing them couldn't really do anything terribly bad to them as long as there were lots of witnesses around, right?

Then she thought again. She thought about how "whatever it was" had invaded the building she'd lived in, a building full to the top with people. How it had broken down her door, and had done something dreadful to her loud and nosy neighbor.

Morgan's heart sank again and she huddled deeper into her oversized jacket. All at once, she didn't feel as safe and secure as she had just a minute ago. She held a bit tighter to the grab rail, and jerked hard on the shoulder strap to pull her over-sized duffle bag a bit closer.

A muffled gasp half mew and half curse rose out of the top of the duffle bag.

"Easy there, Morgan my girl" yelped the cat from his hidden position within the bag.

"This is only soft luggage," he continued more quietly "which means any rigid, hard or pointy thing you find to bang it against also bangs up against the soft and handsome contents. So go easy on that kind of thing."

"Sorry" Morgan gasped, at once contrite. She'd had to hide Sam in the top of her duffle bag to get the both of them onto the down town bus. This was not a totally happy solution for either of them. Not only was the inside of the partially closed bag stuffy and claustrophobic, but this also left him vulnerable to the cavalier way she treated her hand luggage. The cat was distinctly feeling the strain.

"Won't happen again," she said under her breath.

"Better not," grumbled the cat in a low tone. "I've got bruises on my bruises in here, and that interferes with my rugged good looks. What the heck did you pack in here anyway, heavy machinery?"

Morgan thought guiltily for a second about the flashlight, books and spare pair of running shoes she'd thrown into the bag when she was told to pack to run for her life at short notice. If she'd known she was also going to be toting around a talkative and smart assed companion, she might have packed differently.

"Never mind that," she said quickly. "Think our stop's coming up. What's the cross street again?"

From inside of the bag, she heard the sounds of paper crinkling and a bus schedule being opened and refolded.

"Looks like we get off at the corner of Lake Street and Forest Avenue, and cut across the park" her passenger muttered. "In case we were being watched, we didn't want to get off right at our destination. That'd make it too easy for someone or something to follow us."

"Well, we're only five blocks away" said Morgan "so we'd better get ready to get off."

"All right – bracing self" the voice from beyond came back.

"That's fun-ny, cat; very funny indeed..." said Morgan from between clenched teeth. She reached down and scooped up the duffle bag by the strap, doing her best to ignore the sound of "oompf" that came out. She stood up, slung the bag over her shoulder, and began to work her way down the aisle to the front door as the bus drew closer to their stop.

Reaching the front, she crouched slightly and bent towards the driver so she could tell him her stop without others hearing. "Corner of Lake Street and Forest Avenue," she murmured. The driver nodded once.

A moment later, the bus pulled over at the corner, and Morgan and her massive duffle bag struggled down the steep bus stairs to the street. She stepped onto the curb and moved briskly forwards along the shadowed side walk, hauling her luggage along as the bus pulled away into the night.

As the bus moved out, the silence gathered around her as thick and clinging as darkling honey from African killer bees. The dark was soft, mysterious and cool; and the light pulling away with the departing bus suddenly seemed like the last vestiges of safety, the last traces of her familiar life vanishing into the past. Morgan shivered, and huddled into her coat, wrapping it around her like the illusion of her former life.

She adjusted the strap on her shoulder again to make it ride more comfortably for the long walk over to the library

"Oof!" said the bag once again. "I think, all things considered, that I'd prefer to walk for this stage of the trip. Can you let me out please? "

Sighing, she settled the duffle bag gently to the cement and bent to unzip it. Sam stuck his nose out and then emerged from the bag with style and panache, despite the rough ride he'd been having. He sneezed and shook himself once, re-settling himself into a more stylish and reserved persona again and then struck a cat pose for a moment, simply to re assert his dominance on the world that lay around him.

Morgan sighed again, zipped up the bag, and settled it on her shoulder once more. It was much lighter with her companion walking beside her. She looked around the abandoned street corner, trying to decide which direction would be the best one to take to reach the library.

In the distance, the bus stopped again.

The street lights made puddles of light in the darkness of the city, reaching down the street as far as she could see. The wind gusted and whispered, driving pieces of paper down against her ankles and speaking of hidden secrets.

As she looked down the street, she could see that someone get off of the bus, but could not see a face in the shadows. The bus doors clanked and closed again, and the bus pulled off into oblivion. The disembarked rider turned and started slowly walking in their direction.

And something caught her attention about that figure in the distance…

Sam looked up at Morgan, and turned to look in the direction she was facing.

A whistle echoed down the streets–a whistle that seemed to expand to fill the world around them

Sam looked back at Morgan again, and there was a look of panic on his face. "Run!" he shouted.

He pivoted and began to sprint away, and Morgan ran after him.

The whistling echoed down the street behind them, and the echoing sound of footsteps on concrete seemed to expand until whistling and footsteps filled the world with sound. Morgan and Sam ran pell mell, unreasoning panic setting in as they fled from their half seen pursuer.

Down the street they ran, and around the corner, and down another block like lightning; and still the footsteps came closer and closer

Despite the fact that they were running head long and their unseen companion seemed following them at a leisurely walk, the footsteps seemed right behind them, closer and closer, resonating in time with the pounding of their hearts.

Down another block and around another corner and there was the open square and the library beyond it, marble roof gleaming over the central palazzo and flashing through the clump of urban trees in the center of the square.

"Around the edge or through the little woods? Around or through?" Morgan thought frantically

She began to run straight forwards, towards the little grove of trees, but Sam cut across her path and forced her into bypassing the central mini park. As she ran, breath pounding, Morgan noticed the shadows under the trees seemed somehow thicker and darker than they had previously and abruptly more ominous. She was suddenly glad that she'd not run in amongst the trees and found what might be hiding there in the shadows…

And the sound of the whistling was pounding in her ears, filling her with panic

The final stretch now, and around the corner end of the park. The steps to the library were in sight. Heart pounding, breath heaving, Morgan sprinted up the stairs, Sam flashing before her, and ran beneath the shelter of the portico in front of the library doors.

Sam stopped and turned to look at the street below them

In the near distance, at the corner of the edge of the park, they could see the following figure standing, his face still hidden by shadow. A whistle drifted across the air between them. And then the figure turned on his heel and was gone again…

Morgan and Sam stood on the porch of the library, breathing heavily, gasping with exhaustion and trying to get their center back.

"Who was that? What was that?" Morgan finally wheezed, bent almost double as she tried to catch her breath.

"Don't know," said Sam. "Don't want to know. Some things are just better not to know about. But it would have been bad if it caught us…"

"And, in under the trees?" said Morgan. "What...?"

"Another thing I think its better we didn't find out about," said Sam "I think that we were being herded, and I can't think they meant for us to end up in a good place."

They stood for a moment in relative peace, panting in unison until their breathing returned to normal. Then the golden cat turned to look speculatively at the library, having regained his aplomb.

"I'm afraid that I'm going to have to get back into that lousy bag again, if you're going to smuggle me in there" he said thoughtfully…

Twelve
Morgan

The library was a large and impressive building, a remnant of a more glorious and grandiose period in the city's history. Its marble walls, lofty pillars, towering steps and expansive picture windows all spoke of a place where knowledge was honored and treasured, and where all were welcome equally to share in the knowledge gathered by mankind.

Morgan stood outside, contemplating the entryway and planning her approach.

"You'll need to keep your head down while I'm smuggling you in" she said quietly, carefully pulling the zipper a bit more closed, in a manner calculated to avoid catching golden ears or treasured tail.

"I haven't lived here for long, but I've spent enough time in this library to learn about it. Keep quiet until I get you to a quieter section of the library. They're near to closing and they don't check the building that carefully. There are lots of places to hide out in. Once they've shut down for the night, I'll let you out and we can find a place to camp out in until morning."

"I know, I know" griped Sam. "For heavens' sake, you'd think I was unfamiliar with deception. How do you think your tuna sandwiches keep disappearing, anyway? "

Morgan stopped in indignation.

"You fink!" she said. "You mean you're the one who keeps taking my lunch and leaving me with nothing but very healthy fruit to eat?"

A conciliatory voice drifted up from her bag.

"Umm, well, that's not really very important right now" he said. "I swear we'll talk about it some other time when our tails aren't on the line like they are now. Ready to go, Morgan."

Fuming, Morgan stalked up the marble stairs and into the library.

Once inside the massive lobby, Morgan veered left and climbed the spiral stairs to the upper level. Recent experience had taught her the upper stacks were more quiet and isolated, and that she was unlikely to be found if she settled quietly up there. (Indeed a nap attack over a particularly dry and boring book led to her waking with a start when the facility lights were shut off. Since then, she'd carried a pocket flashlight in her purse and another on her key chain for just such occasions.)

At the top of the stairs, she dove deep into the stacks, located an empty leather chair in the hinterlands of world folklore, ("Ironic!" she thought.), and kept quiet as a mouse.

Soon, she heard the familiar sounds of the librarian calling "Last call. The library is closing. This is your last chance to check out any books before we close for the night." She heard the security guard come to the top of the stacks, calling "The library is closing, folks. Time to go home." And patrolling slowly across the fronts of the upper stacks before going back down the other staircase.

She stayed put in her chair, hushed and still.

Then all of the lights went out. And she was sitting in darkness, broken only by reflected glimmers of street lights through the windows below.

Silently, she counted to herself. One. . . two. . .

three. . .

When she reached fifty, she lit the flashlight from her purse, cautiously shielding the bulb so no light would reflect through the windows. She carefully opened the duffle bag to give Sam his freedom.

"Well, it's about time!" complained the golden cat emerging from the duffle bag. "I thought I was going to suffocate in that mess! And what did you have packed in there, anyway? Some of the hardest, lumpiest clothing you own? Next time, I want to ride in style!"

Morgan grinned.

"That's right," she kidded. "I'll run out and get you one of those cushy little tote bags with rhinestones that all the society divas carry their yappy little dogs around in. Your total comfort will be my first and only concern. Of course, I can't really help it if all of your metaphysical buddies laugh their heads off at you."

"Well, maybe not that," he huffed. "But, it surely was uncomfortable and undignified in there. That was no way to treat a cat, especially one of my very distinguished lineage."

She bent down and kissed him fondly on the top of the head.

"I'm sorry, honey" she said, "but sacrifices must be made. We're on the run, and I didn't have much time to prepare for it properly."

The cat tried to keep glowering, but a satisfied grin slid across his face despite his best efforts.

"Oh, that's ok, Morgan" he said. "I know you're doing the best you can under the circumstances."

"Now, make sure to keep quiet and be careful" she

said, changing the subject. "I'm not sure I'm the only person who's thought of this. I can't think of many people who would do it for fun, but there might be some homeless people crashing here or other folks you don't want seeing you."

"Besides that, you need to know that the entrance is flanked with huge glass windows. We know for certain that there are folks out there that neither of us wants to run into, so we want to be sure we're not spotted from outside the library."

"Thanks." said Sam. "I'll just go check this place out for other visitors to avoid."

"And I'll look for a good out of the way place for us to crash." said Morgan. "Once I've got that, I'll stop by the lady's room to get some water for you, and set up supper for two."

"See you in fifteen, then," said Sam. "If you get in trouble, just holler."

"You too, fuzz face," she grinned.

The cat huffed in mock indignation and was gone into the shadows like smoke. She gathered herself more slowly, re-zipping her duffle bag and stopping to consider options before she moved.

Shading her flashlight beam, she explored the library until she found a cozy, sheltered nook, in the back of the stacks, hidden behind a cluster of shelves. Three leather chairs there could be a make-shift bed, and a set of book carts nearby added partial cover for her arrangement from any unlikely person who came that way. The niche was even better because it was at the end of several different aisles between the shelves, so there were multiple escape routes if rapid departure became necessary.

Morgan nodded her head in satisfaction. She'd found a haven for them for the night.

Continuing to shade her flashlight, Morgan crept downstairs to visit the lady's room. Once inside, she turned on the bathroom light and looked at herself in the mirror.

She looked like hell. There were smudges on her face and clothing, her hair was tangled and all a-straggle, her collar was twisted awry, and her hands were grimy. She looked like what her foster mother used to refer to as "who-did- it-and- ran". It was a wonder they had not stopped her at the door of the library.

Morgan sighed deeply, turned on the water, and set down to work…

A good twenty minutes later, she looked back in the mirror and was much more satisfied with the Morgan that she saw. Her tangled hair was once again tamed and smoothed back into some semblance of order. Her face and hands were clean again, scrubbed rigorously until shining to remove any miscellaneous residue left from the unexpected dumbwaiter ride. The spots on her clothing were scrubbed by hand until gone, or at least less noticeable; and her clothing patted dry and straightened so she no longer looked like she'd been out brawling.

In short, her appearance was adequate, and, more importantly, no longer distinctive; and she felt much better having pulled herself together again.

Feeling renewed and refreshed, she filled her water bottle with clear, clean water for them both to drink with dinner. She turned on her flashlight, turned off the lights in the bathroom and cautiously made her way back upstairs.

She reached the chair they'd originally hidden in and found Sam waiting for her.

"Where the heck have you been?" he asked. "I've been waiting for you. The coast is clear. No one in here but us, so we can rest easy for now."

"I've been downstairs in the lady's room cleaning up," she said. "When I stopped to get some water, and got a look at myself in the mirror, I looked like an escapee from an asylum, I thought that it'd be a good idea to straighten myself up so I wouldn't be noticeable and attract unnecessary attention. Besides, it felt so good to have a clean face and hands again."

The cat sputtered in indignation, but before he could say anything, she continued.

"Besides, I've already found us the perfect place to crash. It's secluded, comfortable, and has multiple exit routes to boot! You're gonna love it! Step right this way, oh exalted cat of mine!"

She led him back through the stacks to the sheltered nook. Once they'd arrived, he inspected it carefully and agreed that he hadn't found a better spot in the entire library for them to camp in. Having agreed on a resting spot, Sam supervised as Morgan dug deeply into her bag and pulled out tuna, crackers and cheese, and some snack cakes for dessert. She poured water into his travel bowl, then raised her water bottle in a toast.

"To us" she said. "To a boring journey, and a safe arrival, and, most of all, to a happily ever after."

"To confusion to our enemies, and aid to our friends" Sam replied. "To our wits being sharper, our reactions faster, and our actions fiercer than that of those who oppose us. . ."

" . . . And to a bit of that tuna in oil" he added. "I don't suppose you could pass it over here, could you?"

They feasted then by the shine of her flashlight, safe in the depths of the stacks, and then curled up for the night.

The Lands That Lie Between

Thirteen
Elsewhere

And outside the library walls, Unseelie hunters continued to search for the bearers of the power…

The Lands That Lie Between

Fourteen
Morgan

Morgan awoke with a start, tucked up under her coat on her bed of leather library chairs. She thought she'd heard something, and she listened for all her worth for the noise that had awakened her.

But no noise came.

After a moment, she sat up right, still listening. Still no noise.

Turning on her flashlight, she looked over to where Sam slept. He was still fast asleep, ear flicking as he dreamed, but no signs of alarm in his fuzzy little body.

"If there really was a sound, surely he'd have heard it more quickly than I did." thought Morgan. "He's got great ears. He's more alert. He's here to watch over me. There must not have been a sound. I must have dreamed it."

Relaxing now, she reached for her water bottle to take a sip, only to find she'd drained the last drop hours ago. Parched, she sat up, slid her feet carefully into her shoes, and, taking water bottle and flashlight, carefully and quietly headed down the stairs to the bathroom.

Emerging moments later from the bathroom refreshed and with water bottle refilled, Morgan turned to go back up the stairs. It was then that she noticed the light shining under the door behind the front desk.

"That light wasn't been there before" she thought, mind whirling.

Some one must have turned on the light. Someone must be in there.

Holding her breath, Morgan crept forward and around the edge of the counter. Moving inch by inch until she reached the door, she touched it and nudged it slightly open so she could peek in.

The light inside was cool and clear and luminous. Not surprising, until Morgan looked up and realized that the lighting fixtures were still off.

A pallid and amorphous figure was seated at the desk in the office, bent over a prodigious pile of paperwork. "They always get these requisitions mixed up." It muttered.

Then the figure looked up and smiled warmly. "Come in, come in!" it said "I'm glad you're here. I've been waiting for you!"

Morgan realized that she was looking at a pale but kindly looking woman with glasses. A **transparent** pale but kindly looking woman with glasses…

For a moment, Morgan felt she should be terrified, but she felt at ease. Remembering that her tarot reading spoke of help from unexpected allies, and that she should trust her instincts, Morgan followed her impressions, opened the door fully and walked in.

"I've seen you in the library before" said the translucent woman. "You know books, and you love them. That makes me happy, because I know books and I love them myself."

Suddenly, a look of consternation spread across her pleasant face. "Oh, I'm so sorry," said the woman, "How very discourteous of me –I've not introduced myself. I'm the hearth spirit of this library. You may call me Mary. Mrs. Mary J. Weller was the woman who created this library, and I liked the name so much that I've co-opted it as my own."

She extended her hand to Morgan.

Gingerly, Morgan took her hand and shook it. It was like shaking hands with a moonbeam.

The translucent woman beamed at her, and Morgan felt oddly comforted.

"A hearth spirit? What on earth is a hearth spirit?" she asked curiously.

Mary took off her glasses and tapped them thoughtfully on her hand.

"How best to describe this?" she said. "Try this. When a place is full of people coming and going, if it's just a way station for mankind, it has few defenses against invasion by things supernatural. For example, a vampire can walk into Grand Central Station at any time that he so chooses because that place doesn't energetically belong to any one in particular. It's open territory, and free to all. Do you follow me so far?"

Morgan nodded. "That makes sense."

"When a place has been lived in by a person or a family that loves that place, that love builds up creativity and love and light within it. It's more than a house. It becomes a home. This is true of house/homes, and apartment/homes, and mansion/homes, and shack/homes and any building that becomes a receptacle for love and living-any place that's truly a home."

"Now when a house becomes a home, there's some protection from supernatural elements that accompanies this state. A home protects the people who live there, and resists intrusions by uncanny elements that aren't personally welcomed by the residents. That's why the same vampire who could dance the Charleston in Grand Central Station if he liked, cannot cross the threshold of a home, without being invited in by someone who lives there. Are you still with me?"

Morgan nodded again.

"Finally, in very extreme cases, some places that have been homes for many generations or that accrue extreme amounts of love and community develop what's referred to as a hearth spirit or a spirit of place. The protective elements connected with a home are so strong that they create an actual being that watches over the well-being of those who live there."

"This usually only happens in places where people live, but it has been known in non-residential places in isolated incidents."

"That's where I come in" said Mary cheerfully. "This library is not just a public building. The original Mary Weller was a woman who loved learning and believed deeply in its capacity to work wonders in people's lives. She raised the money to build and stock this library based on the concept of free knowledge for everyone, regardless of financial status or personal back ground. She started programs that have lasted to this day-literacy programs, community meetings, educational opportunities and employment networking and a hundred more."

"And her love for learning, community and the world was contagious, and has changed the nature of this city, inspiring further acts of love and light. With all that love and passion, it's not surprising that this library has a hearth spirit."

"And that's me," she smiled earnestly. "I watch

over the children in the daycare program downstairs. I put the right books in front of eager minds. I connect job seekers with positions. I smooth the waters at community meetings held here. I do a hundred other little things to try to make this community wiser, kinder, more full of hope."

"I also try to straighten out the darned requisition forms" she sighed "but that's still a work in progress..."

"But, enough about me!" Mary continued warmly. "Let me put my librarian hat on here." She straightened slightly and folded her hands. "How can I help you?" she asked in a formal manner.

Morgan was floored. She'd gotten so interested in what Mary was saying she'd completely forgotten about her own situation.

"I don't quite know. . ." she stammered, finding herself suddenly awkward and uncertain. "I'm sleeping here tonight with. . ."

"Your friend, Sam the cat, who you smuggled in by your duffle bag just before closing. You're hiding here because you're being pursued by dangerous elements of the unseelie court who have destroyed your apartment and are trying to eliminate you, to keep you from contributing your part to the power involved in the crowning of the next elven king of the Lands Between." said Mary.

She laughed at the stunned look on Morgan's face. "You know, I'm a reference librarian." She chortled. "We know all of the good stories."

"I guess that you do." said Morgan slowly. "Is there anything that you **can** do to help me?"

"Three things" said Mary cheerfully. "And, since you seem to be caught in an enchanted adventure story, three is a powerful and quite proper number."

"First, I will ensure that nothing will harm you, no matter how powerful it may be, as you sleep in the library tonight. You're safe here, but you can't stay here, for your mission has a deadline and if you don't reach your goal in time, things will go badly, not only for you, but for the world of humankind."

"Second, I've a book here that includes maps of all of the infrastructure of the city, including streets and alleys, sewer ways, cross-throughs and even a few concealed passageways. This might help you arrive where you need to go. You're approved to check this book out for up to two weeks, but I expect you to return it in good condition within the allotted time."

"And if you do not return this book on time and in good condition, I will hunt you down and haunt you until you do." Mary twinkled.

"And thirdly, I've something here that has been waiting for someone like you."

Mary reached into a drawer in the desk, and pulled out a tiny jar.

"This is a very small container of an ointment that'll let you see into enchantment. Rub this into your eyes, and you'll see not only physical reality, but also metaphysical as well. Illusions will be stripped away. True forms will be revealed. The gates to the Lands Between will be visible to you. You'll be able to see auras, and healing energy, magickal spells and the glow that shines from those active in the mystic arts."

"I've been saving it for someone special, and it looks like you're her." smiled Mary.

"Thank you." said Morgan, taking her gifts in wonder. "You've been so kind. No wonder I always love coming here."

Mary smiled. "It's well you've come to see me when you did," she said kindly. "I'm always here, but there are only a few times when you can talk with me directly. We're just fortunate that you happened by during one of those times. Now hurry off and sleep well, my dear. Nothing will disturb you while I'm on duty."

"And when your adventure is over" she added "do come back and tell me all about it. I do love a good fantasy adventure tale."

Morgan flew out of the office door and up the steps to wake Sam, and tell him what had happened.

"Urrr, Arr, Ummm" he grumbled, stumbling back to consciousness. "Don't be silly. There are no hearth spirits in libraries, only in very special homes."

"But this is a **very** special library." Morgan insisted. "You have to meet her."

Still grumbling, he followed her back downstairs; but when they reached the front desk, the room behind it was dark and there was no one to be seen.

"See? You just dreamed it." Sam grumbled.

Morgan thrust the little jar into his face. "Did I just dream this?" she asked.

Sam looked at the jar for a moment, and blinked. A look of wonder came over his furry countenance.

"The ointment of enchanted Sight!" he gasped. "Where the heck did you get your hands of the ointment of

65

enchanted Sight?

    "Ha!" she said. And then, she told him. . . .

Fifteen
Elsewhere

She was strong and fierce and powerful. Her eyes were keen, missing nothing; her wing span was wider than a tall man could reach; and her sharp talons and powerful jaws had made more than one unseelie threat reconsider his plans, turn tail and head for far greener pastures, ones easier to conquer. Her cunning, courage and martial prowess made her more than a fit guardian for the spark of power that she carried within her; and normally, she would have no fear, knowing herself more than a match for anything unseelie sent against her.

Yet, for once, she felt uneasy. . .

Arcing through the concrete canyons of the city, eyes peeled and ears at the ready for any possible danger, she mentally soothed herself as she flew.

Soon she would be home in the halls of Light. Soon her precious cargo would be delivered and safe. Soon she would arrive and prepare for the crowning of a new king-a king of Light.

And the spears of lightning flying up from her path below caught her unawares; plunging into her in wing and breast and belly...

Screaming madly, she crashed to earth.

A crowd of massive little figures leaped out of the shadows and fell upon her with knives.

Very sharp knives...

The screaming continued, but only for a little while longer.

And when the police arrived there, summoned by

many phone calls from surrounding buildings, there was no sign that anything had happened, or that she'd ever even existed. . .

Sixteen
Morgan

Morgan and Sam had talked late into the night, before finally returning to their improvised beds. Sam had immediately recognized the ointment that Mary had given Morgan, although it was so rare and precious that he had never actually seen it before. He was also very familiar with the use of it, and with ancient stories of how best to use it to their mutual advantage.

"This special ointment is hard to make and hard to come by" Sam said, "and, from what I've heard, different batches have different lengths of effectiveness. For the most part, it wears off, although I've heard stories of some batches that were actually permanent. Still, unless we've reason to believe otherwise, we should assume that a dab of this will only give you the Sight for a finite time, and act according to that idea."

"Furthermore, since one of its qualities is to let you to see through all illusions and eleven glamours, there's a basic problem here. If you only see what truly is, you won't be reacting to things as other people see them, and that can cause a whole different bunch of problems."

"The best way around these issues" said Sam "is to only put the ointment in one eye. If you do that, you'll still be able to see the things ethereal, but you'll be able to determine what's physical reality, and what's magickal reality by opening and closing the eye you've treated. And that'll also mean that you use the ointment up more slowly, so that it'll last longer."

"That makes sense." Morgan agreed. "Since my

right eye's dominant, I'll put the ointment in my left one. That'll mean that, when both of my eyes are open, I'll see both physical and metaphysical worlds, and when I close my left eye, I'll only see the physical world, which will help me navigate like normal people. Have I got that right?"

Sam nodded. "Of course, you'll have to watch out for uncanny threats that think that you're winking at them." He teased. "You might even get a date out of this."

Morgan huffed at him and stuck out her lower lip. "That's quite enough commentary about my dating habits." She said sternly. "Time enough to think about my social life once we get through all of this- if we do, of course."

"And did you take a look at this book?" she continued. "Look at all the alleyways and cross-throughs and roads that I had no idea existed. This could really be a blessing to us! Show me where we're going and let's pick out the best route and an alternate to get there."

Sam bent his head over the central map in the book. "You're right. This is amazing. I thought I knew all there was to know about the highways, byways and paths Between in this area, but there are roads here I don't think anyone knows these days."

"Let me think" said Sam. "Our destination is here" he indicated with one furry paw, "but we must enter at this point to properly attend the gathering of the bearers of the power. We could take this route" he pointed "which seems pretty simple, but if things start to get hot, we could dodge this way, or that way, or that way over there, to avoid as many hostile receiving parties as possible. Do you see how we're getting there?"

"I do" said Morgan "but have you considered going round about here? I must admit that the term "secret tunnel" just speaks to me" she grinned.

"True enough, true enough." Sam grinned back "but short, quick and by them before they know that we're coming is still the best option. We can keep that in reserve for emergencies, though."

Their plans made and their hearts lightened, they lay back down again to catch what little sleep they could before the library opened once more in the morning.

The Lands That Lie Between

Seventeen
Elsewhere

Foot steps rang out on the pavement-foot steps running frantically, and far too many other footsteps in hot pursuit behind. A figure careened wildly around a corner in the dark, running desperately towards the brilliant lights of the mall in the distance.

If he could only reach those lights. If he could only reach those people-it'd be far too public for those pursuing him. They would not be able to do anything so obvious in front of the humans. He would be safe for the moment, and maybe even have a chance to think of something, to pull one more last trick out of his bag of many illusions.

And then, the footsteps behind him caught up with him- and turning, struggling, fighting, he went down. . . .

The Lands That Lie Between

Eighteen
Morgan

In the morning, the sunlight poured in through the big front windows like honey. Sam and Morgan awoke, well rested despite their evening's activities. They returned the nook to its previous setup. Who knew if they might have to use it again?

They looked around for Mary, but didn't find her, though they knew she must be there somewhere.

Morgan went downstairs to the lady's room to change brush her teeth and her hair, and fill her water bottle for later. Drinking deeply, she looked into the mirror and was pleased with what she saw. Nothing extraordinary. Nothing that stood out in the slightest. Nothing that could possibly indicate to the casual observer that she was, in reality, (Ba Ba Ba!) A Mythic Heroine in a Dramatic Adventure in the Overlap Between Fantasy and Reality!!!

She struck a heroic pose for a minute, and then collapsed giggling, obscurely cheered in some manner. Still giggling, she thoroughly cleaned her hands and carefully took the tiny jar from the inner pocket of her purse. Gingerly, she took a scant finger full of the ointment and dabbed it in to her left eye.

It stung. Boy, did it sting. Morgan danced around the bathroom, cussing, her eye tearing up.

And then, her vision cleared. . . .

The room around her seemed brighter, full of light. She closed her left eye and the light returned to how she remembered it. Opening her eye and looking down, she saw the ointment in the jar shone brightly, like ground up stars. Hastily, she recapped it, and tucked it back away in her purse pocket, pleased to see that the light did not show through jar and purse.

She heard the sound of a tail being emphatically thumped against the bathroom door.

"What the blazes are you doing in there?" shouted Sam sarcastically. "Dying your hair? Complete makeover? Are you going to be in there all day? The library is going to open up soon, and we'll need to be out of sight before that happens, your highness!"

Morgan opened the door sharply. Sam stood there, glowing slightly in her altered sight.

"Hold your horses, fuzzy face," she said sharply but playfully. "A lady's got just a few little things that she needs to take care of in the morning, you know. Now, are you going to need some of this ointment?"

"I don't need it!' he said smugly. "Cats can already see into the mystical as well as the physical. Cats are really special that way."

"Well, I guess that I'm just really lucky to have such a very special guy on the road with me" she grinned at him. "Come on, buddy. Let's go hide out before they open the doors and catch us."

They climbed the spiral staircase one more time and burrowed deep into the upper stacks to the reading areas. Morgan took a book on ancient folk lore on fairies to read, and Sam took a cat nap as they waited patiently for the library doors to open and for enough time to pass to permit them to drift out again unnoticed.

Several hours later, the library had opened and enough traffic had developed for Morgan to exit, with Sam once more tucked up in her duffle bag.

"Leave the bag more open" he suggested. "If things get busy, I'm going to need to be able to move without you struggling with fasteners."

"Why would things possibly be getting busy in the daylight?" she scoffed. "The creepy things only come out at night, right?"

"Not so, my darling" Sam said. "There are plenty of very bad things that can happen to you well before the sun goes down. Not only do you have all of the normal hazards and obstacles to be concerned about, but a certain amount of unseelie activity is also on the move in the daytime."

This was a new idea to Morgan. She didn't like it much.

"Remember" said Sam "that magickal beings are alive and well and moving about amongst you humans and also that the fae want to conceal the existence of the Lands Between, because that knowledge puts them at risk from humanity, both individually and as a world. That's all they want to conceal. If they can keep their nature concealed and get away with nefarious activities as well in the process, many fae, especially unseelie, will do it. You can certainly get mugged in daylight, and that includes getting mugged by unseelie goons wearing an elven glamour that makes them look like mortals."

"A glamour..?" asked Morgan.

"A glamour is a kind of spell that makes a person look different than he or she really is. Often elven glamours not only conceal the natures of those wearing them, but also make them more attractive to the people around them, even to the point of being able to influence or control the behavior of others." Sam said. "The ointment of enchanted Sight gives you the ability to see through glamours to the true form-but only if you chose to look."

"I guess that the point I'm trying to make here is you're much safer in daylight hours, but only because there are some unseelie that stand out in good lighting, and because it's easier to conceal ill-doing after dark." said Sam. "This safety, however, is definitely only relative: bad things can still happen in the daylight."

"And speaking of daylight "said Sam "time's wasting! Let's hit the bricks and cover some major ground before something catches up to us!"

Thoughtfully, Morgan headed out on the route that they had chosen together.

Nineteen
Morgan

They'd made some distance but had to duck into shops they were passing on multiple occasions to hide, and diverged from their chosen pathway because Morgan spotted distant figures with an unearthly glow using the enchanted Sight in her left eye.

By now it was late morning, and the detours and hiding had left them hours off of their expected schedule and miles from their original route.

Morgan sat at an outdoor table of a coffee shop, sipping a mocha, feeding scraps of a chicken salad sandwich to her duffle bag, and pouring frantically over the various maps in the book, looking for an alternative route.

"Mmmm, that's really yummy." murmured the bag. "How about little bit more of that sandwich, then?"

"Will you hush up, please?" Morgan snapped. "Focus! I'm trying to find a workable route to the court, and all you can think about is your stomach!"

"A hero needs his strength," said the duffle bag. "I'm just trying to keep my strength up to par so I can be ready to face whatever befalls us."

"Well, a heroine needs her strength, too," said Morgan "and remember, half of that sandwich is mine. Now, will you focus and help me here?"

"Well, drop the book lower, so I can get a better look at it. Maybe if you'd do that, I could contribute," said the bag.

"Remember that the official gateway we're headed for is only open between noon and midnight today. Once the clock strikes midnight, that gate closes, and nothing official's open until a different gate opens tomorrow at noon. Inconvenient, I know, but someone got the idea at some point that it keeps out the riff raff and they've been doing it that way ever since. You know elves and tradition."

"Actually, I don't really. . ." said Morgan uncertainly, but Sam rambled on without a pause.

"While there are lots of gates that open at various times for different purposes, as an official heir and a carrier of power, you're obligated to enter at the official gate at the right time or your role becomes null and void, the official wyverns consume you whole, and the paperwork is unbelievable," the bag continued in Sam's voice.

"Actually I'm kidding about the official wyverns," he said. "but certainly not the paperwork."

"For this reason, we've no choice but to choose a route that goes to the official gate during the right hours. We should try to make it today, but if that gets too sticky, we've got one more day to get there in time for the selection and crowning of the new king."

"Taking a look here, how about cutting across Leister Square, down Cockleberry lane, and through that aperture marked "Secret passage" to get us somewhat back on track? You did say that you wanted to use a secret passage." Sam coaxed.

Morgan looked at the path described. Perfect! They were still running far behind, but the path in question might possibly help them make up some of the time.

"That looks great!" she said in surprise. "Why didn't I see it before?"

She'd never seen a duffle bag look smug before, but somehow, this one managed.

" It's all part and parcel of the magnificent wisdom of cats" said the bag "now, could you just pass a little bit more of that delicious **hero** sandwich down here, hmm?"

She smacked the paw extending out of the bag and reaching for the rest of her lunch. Breaking off a controlled portion and feeding it to the bag, she took the remainder and rose, setting out once more.

The Lands That Lie Between

Twenty
Elsewhere

Miles away, in the countryside beyond the city, the hunt was on. Hounds with red eyes bayed and raced across the fields, howling after their prey.

The fox ran flat out, twisting through the underbrush, doubling back through thickets, breaking her scent on stone and in water. She ran with all the hunt sense of her thousand years of wisdom.

She dashed along a stone wall which would not hold her scent. She doubled back across her own trail, muddling the track. She used a deadfall tree as a platform for a mighty leap, leaving a trail that ended.

And then she hid. And watched.

And this time, the hounds went by.

"Hounds" the fox thought. "They never learn."

And she set off once more for the eleven court.

The Lands That Lie Between

Twenty-One
Morgan

It was when they were crossing Leister Square that things went seriously wrong.

The square was a open area, with a beautiful little city park in the center of it, surrounded by a bustling traffic circle, with lots of foot traffic and cars entering and leaving the circle. "Very public, very safe looking." Morgan thought as she cut straight across the middle through the blossoming fruit trees.

Which suddenly turned and opened fire.

Blasts of energy, ugly energy with a sick and poisonous color, were cutting through the air and flying towards her.

Morgan froze in shock. A bolt of muddy fire struck her, searing her nerve endings with pain, burning her arm, and throwing her bodily to the ground.

Time stood still for just a second.

Morgan closed her right eye, and saw that, in the place of some of the trees were wizened crone-like women, pointing rough twigs from which the energy blasts flew.

Magick wands.

Morgan closed her left eye and opened her right. No women to be seen now, only fruit trees. No blasts of energy, only a woman with a duffle bag sprawled on the ground. No one passing in the physical world could see what was happening in the metaphysical one, and the presence of witnesses would not prevent any harm to her.

Time unfroze. . .

And Sam came leaping like thunder out of the

duffle bag.

In the sight of her left eye, he seemed larger now, stronger, more savage, more dangerous. Sam flew through the air and pounced upon one of wizened women. Seizing her wand in his mouth, he bit it fiercely in two, before turning to claw wildly at a second woman. In a trice, a third one was tumbling on the ground at his paws and he was still accelerating as he brought mayhem into their midst.

Then a poisonous blast struck him hard in the chest, and he went down.

The hags were on him at once, clutching with bony fingers, striking out with their fists, and clawing at his skin. There were so many of them that they interfered with each other for a moment, and he took every advantage that he got, struggling and biting and clawing until at last they bore him down with sheer numbers.

Morgan scrambled to her feet to help him. Sam's eyes met Morgan's from across the square.

"Run for it, Morgan!" he roared like a lion. "Run! If you love me at all, then run, girl!"

She hesitated for a moment, and then ran. He wanted her safe and able to reach the elven courts. He'd sacrificed himself to give her this chance. If she didn't run, his sacrifice would be wasted.

The sounds of the brawl from the square fell away behind her, but to her horror, she could still hear the sounds of footsteps pounding on the pavement behind her. Rapid footsteps. . .

Morgan ran like the wind, and the pack ran after her. . .

Twenty-Two
Morgan

Morgan dashed across three lanes of traffic, with tears streaming down her face, footsteps pounding on the pavement behind her in fierce pursuit, and the memory of Sam's furry face disappearing beneath a pile of flailing limbs. Car horns beeped furiously behind her, and brakes squealed, as she threw herself up the stairs and through the big brass doors of the department store on the square.

She could hear the footsteps coming pounding behind her. Glancing in the reflection in the door, she saw that she'd left the tree woman behind, but had collected a pack of tall, athletic looking men with serious, intent faces. Squinting for a moment as she ran, she saw a certain pointedness to the ears, a certain cast of features alien to human kind.

Elves. Full sidhe. And on her tail and gaining fast.

And closing her left eye showed her only the group of handsome men that people around her saw moving briskly into the store. No hearth spirit here. The swinging doors barely slowed them down as they followed her in.

Turning the corner, she broke left almost immediately, and took cover behind a holiday display. She'd been in here earlier this week to start her Christmas shopping, and had spent some time enjoying the classic, old-fashioned layout of the building. Moving quickly, she cornered again, and swept behind another festive display,

Quietly, she crouched down low and passed across the room to the far side of a series of counters. By now, she'd crossed her own path at least three times, leaving false trails that should take some time to unravel.

She could hear the sidhe hunters, spreading out in all directions, looking for her. . .

She could feel the sidhe hunters, fierce, intent, with but a single goal-to hunt her down and end her. . .

And she almost froze again in that moment.

But then, she thought of Sam...

Quickly, silently, she moved across the store in a semi-crouch, dodging hunters as she went, until she reached her goal-the women's department.

Crouching so she was sheltered behind the counters, she crawled until she reached a saleswoman, one who looked older and more competent than most of the girls she'd seen. She reached up and tugged at the hem of the saleswoman's jacket.

"Ma'am" she whispered frantically "ma'am, can you please help me? I'm being stalked. I just broke up with my boyfriend last week and he's not taking it well. He and a bunch of his friends have chased me into this store and they're trying to find me."

The saleswoman was startled. She looked down and saw the face of an honestly frightened woman, face crusted with tears, crouched behind the counter with her. Her face softened for a moment, and then her jaw set.

"Of course" she murmured, sotto voce. "Just follow me. I'll keep you safe. Don't worry."

She turned and walked to the hall of dressing rooms. She'd good eyes, and consistently kept her body between Morgan and all of the hunters she spotted. Morgan scurried after her, terrorized; and was amazed when they arrived at their destination safely.

In the hall, Morgan could stand up to walk. The saleswoman took her down to the dressing room at the end of the hall, near the exit door.

"My daughter went through the same thing last year" she said "and we're lucky there was someone to help her when she needed it. You should be safe here-men aren't permitted in these changing rooms, so they'd be pretty obvious; and I'm going to set the security guard on them to keep them occupied."

"Just in case, though, if things start to go badly, I'm going to disable this alarm back here so you can slip out the back without triggering it." She said. "I hate bullies, and I hope you get a restraining order against him and slap his skinny behind in jail. Now are you going to be ok, honey?"

Morgan, speechless at so much kindness, nodded.

"Well that's good." said the saleswoman. "I'd better get back out there so I don't make this obvious. And I'll get Nathaniel on their case. He can give someone grief better than anyone I've ever met."

The saleswoman looked at her for a moment, and then gently touched her cheek. "You take care, honey." She said, then turned and walked back into the store.

Morgan huddled into herself in the dressing room, taking advantage of the breathing space to regain her center; wrapping her arms around herself to try to keep from falling apart.

The sorrow she felt from abandoning Sam threatened to overwhelm her-and yet she couldn't let it do so. Leaving Sam behind, especially in such a situation, felt like betrayal, but she knew it was what he wanted her to do. Still, although the power she bore back to the court meant more than either Sam's or her well being, she still felt like a coward for leaving him.

He could be hurt. He could be **DEAD.** And she'd abandoned him to his fate. . .

Her eyes filled with tears. She'd left him. He'd told her to leave him, but still it didn't feel right.

She knew, though, that Sam would have wanted her safe. Would have wanted her to reach the elven courts.

She couldn't let him down. Sam had sacrificed his life so that she could escape and complete the quest that they had set out together to fulfill; and she couldn't give way now to sorrow and let that sacrifice be for nothing.

As she struggled to pull herself back together, she heard shouting in the store itself.

She took another deep breath, and then slipped out of the changing room. Moving quietly, she moved back down to the end of the passage, back tight against the wall so she could peer into the store without being seen by anyone there.

The security guard was standing in front of a mass of assembled elven hunters; his back stiff, his posture belligerent. Looking through her right eye, Morgan saw a mass of very handsome young men, dressed in high fashion clothing. Looking through her left eye, the pointy ears and openly carried weapons of her pursuers filled her with fear.

"You can't just come barging in to this store, pushing customers aside and making a ruckus." He said again, raising his voice further. "This store is for customers, not for hooligans. You gentlemen will have to leave and leave **now.**"

The bulk of the hunters protested, growled, waved

their arms and otherwise made their displeasure clear.

Then the tallest hunter at the front of the pack spoke and everything changed. The store fell silent. The other elves stopped talking. Even the guard froze for a moment, and Morgan could feel a shift in the air, a tingling in the energy around her, and a sense of subtle, but irresistible pressure.

"Why, of course you're right, my dear sir" said the leader. "This store is for people prepared to buy things; and we are here to do so. My apologies for my party's bad behavior-we were so excited by all of the wondrous things for sale here that we temporarily lost track of our manners. But we're all sorry –**aren't we gentlemen?**"

"Of course…", "Sorry…", "my apologies…" and variations thereof flew out of the pack, in response to the leader's glare.

"And now," said the leader, pulling out an impeccable wallet "we are prepared to buy…"

And Morgan could feel the pressure around her increase.

The guard's posture gradually relaxed, an almost silly grin appearing on his face. The clerks around him also relaxed, although Morgan's clerk continued to have a skeptical look on her face.

And the pack began to hunt again, although more subtly. . .

"Oh, no" thought Morgan "a glamour. An elven glamour. Sam said a good enough glamour could not only deceive people, but also make them do what you want."

Carefully, she eased her way back down the hall towards the exit door. Alarm disengaged, she was able to open it silently. She began to ease out as quietly as she could...

She heard the clerk's voice, shouting "Stop, sir! You can't go down there! Those dressing rooms are for women only-and men are <u>not</u> allowed!" She heard the security guard shout "Stop right there!" foggy as if awakening from a dream.

And then she heard the shots.

Morgan took to her heels and ran for her life...

Twenty-Three
Elsewhere

He was very small. He was a hob, and, while not the least of the sidhe, he was certainly not amongst the greatest of them. His legs were short and his journey long, and that was a hard combination indeed.

Furthermore, he had made a very late start of things. This, together with the length of his stride, had put him well behind most of the other heirs on his journey to the court.

He had heard rumors, too. Rumors about heirs who vanished, who set out and never arrived or who suddenly could not be found in their accustomed haunts. These rumors concerned him, almost to the point of cancelling his journey.

Almost, but not quite.

He set his jaw. Though the rumors concerned him, he could not let them keep him from doing what was right. He had a responsibility, and, frightened or no, he was sworn to go to the court of the Lands Between for the crowning of the new king.

He walked on, a very little figure in a very big world.

His ears twitched, and twitched again. He had heard the rumors, but now he heard something more.

Footsteps. The sounds of something on his trail.

Looking around, he saw a tiny little hole in the wall. A hole barely big enough to hold him as he crept into it.

And waited…

And listened…

The Lands That Lie Between

As the footsteps grew closer and closer...

Twenty-Four
Morgan

...Morgan took to her heels and ran for her life, the door slamming loudly shut behind her.

Evidently the sales clerk had bought her some time, and the security guard with her. Morgan just hoped no one was hurt in the process.

Her muscles burned like fire and her breath came in ragged little gasps as she tapped into athletic depths that she'd never previously realized were in her. By the time this thing was over with, she'd be able to try out for the Olympic team.

"A gun!" she thought as she ran. "I heard a gun! Can freaking elves have guns? Wouldn't that violate some kind of obscure fantasy code of conduct or other? Could that cost them some kind of weird elven style points?"

Still running, she laughed breathlessly. Shortness of breath was making her dizzy.

She kept running, skated around a few corners, and made her path a winding one to make herself harder to follow. The twilight closed in around her, and the shadows offered hope of concealment as she ran, ran, ran.

For a moment, all she could hear as she ran was her own gasps, and the sound of her feet pounding furiously against the pavement. Then she heard the sounds of feet behind her. Many feet. Feet running hard. Feet coming up fast-faster than she could run.

Feet overtaking her.

Morgan reached down further into her depths and emerged with a burst of speed that surprised her.

Unfortunately, the feet following her were even faster.

They were going to catch her. . .

And now, she could hear a motorcycle coming from up ahead.

"Can elves ride motorcycles?" she thought fuzzily as she ran. "Is that another hunter coming towards me?"

"Or maybe it's a human. Maybe they won't hurt me in front of him; but if there's just one human, maybe they'll just kill him too. After all, it's not a popularity contest. They just want to keep their existence secret."

"If I ask for help, I might just get him killed. Maybe I should just let him ride on by…"

The motorcycle burst into view, a classic Harley dwarfed by the enormous biker astride it. His leathers, boots and biking helmet concealed his appearance from the observing eye, but his massive size almost made the solid frame beneath him seem small and dainty.

"A giant!" Morgan thought hysterically. "First brownies, then talking cats, then elves, then hearth spirits and, now, a giant! When I wander into a fairy tale, I don't do it halfway."

Though short of oxygen from running, Morgan had enough breath left to decide that she didn't want to involve an innocent bystander in her situation. She chose to run by the motorcycle, and hope she escaped her pursuers.

What she hadn't planned on was an innocent bystander involving himself in her situation. . .

Morgan swerved to the side to run past the cycle, hoping it would cause her pursuers to scatter. The cyclist swerved too, coming up onto the sidewalk in a rush and straight at her, like a rolling wall of black leather.

At the very last minute, the biker veered slightly. Morgan felt an arm like an iron bar lock around her waist, knocking all of the wind out of her and sweeping her off of her feet and onto the bike, which continued to speed forwards.

Onto the bike-well, sort of. Morgan could feel the ground passing very rapidly near her feet, legs, arms, and various other portions of her anatomy. Far nearer to her anatomy than she was at all comfortable with. She closed her eyes tight and held what breath she had left.

Then she was seated on the bike in front of the immense biker, with no idea whatsoever how she'd gotten there.

There was a roar and a shriek, and Morgan's eyes flew open just in time to see the faces of elven hunters at point blank range; shocked, angry and scattering for their lives as the motorcycle barreled through them.

The elves ran after the bike, but there was no catching it on foot. Morgan heard them cursing, then heard their cursing fade as they fell behind.

The biker pressed something, and the bike horn sounded a rude little toot as they faded into the distance.

And Morgan rode off into the night, in the custody of a mysterious, gigantic, faceless stranger.

The Lands That Lie Between

Twenty-Five
Elsewhere

The hob had huddled for as long as he could in the hole, holding his breath and making himself as small as he could to avoid discovery. He knew somehow that the steps outside did not belong to any kindly beings, earthly or no.

He had avoided detection for some time by his size and his silence, but many kinds of hunters came and went through the alley and he didn't have any chance to escape from his hiding place.

At last, there came hunters fleet of foot and keen of nose, who knew both he and the place he was hidden with but a breath. Paws stretched into the hole, catching at his waist coat and ripping at his skin, until, at last, they hooked him free from his hiding place.

In a flash, he was running-running quite literally for his life, and also for the power and the potential he carried within him.

Behind him he heard a howl go up, a fearsome howl that leant wings to his feet.

He ran through the darkness with death on his heels...

The Lands That Lie Between

Twenty-Six
Morgan

Ten minutes later, Morgan found herself sitting at a table in a tiny tea shop, a cup of soothing chamomile tea in one hand, a delicate but excellent curried chicken salad sandwich in the other. She bit into the sandwich, focusing on the sweet green grapes and chewy cashews in the curried chicken to cover her growing anxiety.

Across the tiny table from her, the mysterious biker placed his own two sandwiches and an extra large cup of steaming Oolong, black on the table and sat down like a small mountain settling, carefully maneuvering himself to fit into the tiny chair in the small space available in the corner of the shop. The darkened faceplate of his helmet still concealed his face.

He was very large, and his current surroundings made him look even larger. What was he anyway? An elven assassin? An ogre ? A crazed human biker? Some nightmare creature from the realms of horror?

And why had he taken her? For what nefarious purpose had he braved the threat of elven hunters to carry her away with him?

Morgan wondered if she should scream for help. She wondered if she **could** scream for help, with the fear she felt at the moment.

Would someone help her? Could they actually help in time, before this mysterious biker snapped her neck, devoured her alive or did whatever it was he had in mind when he'd stolen her away? Would she just put other people in harm's way if she screamed for help?

Morgan took a deep breath…

The biker removed his helmet. Underneath there was no giant, no ogre, no nightmare eldritch horror, no elven hit man. No Hollywood style biker type for that matter. The tarot reader she'd gotten her first reading from looked more like a biker than this fellow did.

His face was round, mild and affable, but with a solid jaw, hinting at more resolve than one might originally guess. His hair was a tousled wreath of gold and brown curls, ringing wildly but genially around his high forehead and intelligent features. Blue-grey eyes blinked at her mildly through silver aviator glasses, studying her carefully for a moment before crinkling at the edges as their owner grinned at her.

He had a grin like a cartoon bear…

He took off his leather gloves, revealing strong, massive hands, with tell-tale scars and calluses that told a story of hard work, and lots of it. He towered over her, but still managed to look friendly, folksy and, well, huggable.

Without the mask of his helmet, the biker seemed an amiable man; one of amazing size, but still just a man.

He looked rather tired, actually. . .

"So, how's the sandwich, then?" he asked mildly. "It's been pretty good when I've had it before, so it seemed a fairly safe bet, not knowing your tastes. I must admit though that the amount of curry in the chicken varies widely, dependent upon the cook's mood."

"And do you have enough tea?" he added. "I tend towards the giant economy vat of caffeinated bliss, but not everyone has my capacity for oceans of oolong, so I thought we'd start you with a normal sized cup. There's more to be had if you want it, though. There's milk, lemon or sugar over at the counter, if you like such things. The air outside's bitterly chill, and you have the look of someone out running around in it for hours, so I thought you'd benefit from getting on the outside of a nice cup of warm liquid."

He looked at her kindly and inquiringly, awaiting her response to the small but sumptuous feast he'd brought her.

Morgan looked at him, goggle-eyed. The contrast between the uncanny experiences she'd recently had and this very mundane meal was severe. For a minute, she felt like she was going to break out into hysterical laughter.

Then she exhaled quietly and relaxed a bit.

She didn't think she was going to have to scream for help after all. She took another bite of sandwich, and sipped her tea.

The biker laughed kindly as he saw her relax.

"Don't think I'm some kind of boogey man anymore?" he grinned. "I know I'm bigger than the average guy, but I'm still a long way off from the kind of nasty folk that were chasing you. Sorry to mix in like that, but I can't stand to see a damsel in distress, so I thought I'd just interfere a bit with their idea of fun."

"By the by, are you all right? I had to grab you fairly hard to make sure that all of you ended up on the bike, and people have been known to get bruises from my portable air lift."

Morgan started. Did he realize that he'd just saved her from elves? For that matter, was he something more than the affable large man he seemed?

Morgan closed her right eye.

Through enchanted sight, her dinner companion seemed larger, if that were possible. His ears were slightly pointed, and he shone with a silvery light focused in the middle of his chest.

An elf! Morgan looked downwards, trying to conceal that she'd seen anything.

As she did, she noticed a smaller silver light at her heart, echoing the larger light across from her.

Was that light the power that she was carrying? That would mean that the biker was another one of the heirs that carried the power of the summer king to the court. But was he seelie or unseelie?

She looked up, her right eye still closed. The biker looked at her quizzically for a moment, and then winked roguishly back at her.

"I'm flattered by the attention from such a pretty lady" he grinned merrily "but I think that my own lady might have something to say about it."

"Seelie," her gut said emphatically. "This man is not an evil menace. A menace, maybe-evil definitely no."

The big biker took a massive bite of curried chicken salad, and followed it with an enormous swig of tea. He then eyed her speculatively over his sandwich.

"So. . ." he started slowly. "What's a nice lady like you doing being chased by idiots like that anyway? Now, I'm good if that's your idea of fun, but you didn't look like you were enjoying yourself. So, I was wondering..?"

Morgan screwed up her courage.

"So you want to know why I was being hunted by

elves..?" she asked.

The biker's eyes went wide. He snorted, and choked on his tea. Morgan had to put in several moments of back pounding before order was restored, which was tricky in the tight quarters of the tea shop.

Everyone turned to look at the hullabaloo. In a moment, the biker recovered himself.

"Nothing to see, folks" he said waving at them, tears flowing down his cheeks."Just some curry that was a bit more exciting than I was prepared for."

Everyone turned back to their own business. The biker dropped his voice and narrowed his eyes, bending closer to Morgan across the table.

"Well, you're a plain spoken one, aren't you?" he hissed. "Ix –nay on the elve-nay talk, sister. It alarms the general population and the pointy eared folk aren't wild about it, either."

"You're a bit pointy, yourself" she hissed back, exasperated. "And I'm not quite sure why you're treating me to really good sandwiches, rather than trying to run me down or hack me up like most of the other sidhe that I've run into. Let's call a spade a spade, here. What are your plans for me? Why did you whisk me away from the hunt pursuing me? And where do you fit in all of this court carrying on?"

The biker looked at her and then threw back his head and laughed loudly. Peoples' heads turned again.

"Plain spoken, indeed" he whispered, tears from choking and laughter still on his face. "Haven't seen one like you for many a year, and it tickles me. Now, in no particular order-I snatched you out from out in front of the hunt because you were in trouble, and I do hate to see a lady in trouble. And because those unseelie bastards have been running down seelie heirs all over the town, and it pleased me to thwart their plans and vex them. And because they've been hunting me, and it gives me joy to pop up, tweak their noses, and to disappear again. And because the more of us make it to court, the more likely this world will continue to be worth living in."

"Where do I fit in?" he asked. "More to the point, do you know where you fit in? I don't have the Sight, but, from the way that pack was carrying on, I'd say you're probably one of the heirs. Would I be right?"

Morgan nodded, indignation fled as fast as it had come.

"Well, I'm also entrusted with a small bit of the power of kings and the calling to bring it back home to court again. And, for some unknown reason" he smiled "I seem to be a more noticeable target for unseelie interference than some of my fellows are. There are absolute swarms of mystical menaces with my name painted on them, to the point that we're going to have to vacate this excellent but tiny tea shop very shortly, before it fills up with the fae and the roof blows right off."

"Which brings me to my plans for you, little sister." He smiled kindly.

Morgan tensed. Now she'd hear the catch.

"My plans for you are basically…nothing. I pulled you out of your predicament because you needed help, because I could give it, and because it is in my nature to tweak the noses of the forces of Darkness" he grinned. "I'd love to let you ride with me to court if you wanted, but truth be told, I'm far more visible than you, and, if you stayed with me, it would only put you more fully in harm's way. So my plan for you is to feed you well, check to see if you're all right, and then get away from you as quickly as possible, so as to keep you safe."

"You are all right, aren't you?" he asked.

This was not at all what Morgan had expected to hear. Her mind whirled.

She paused a moment to think about whether, relatively speaking, she was all right, then nodded.

"Good" beamed the biker. "Then I'll be hitting the road, before I draw them down on you."

He drained his cup of tea and stuffed his second sandwich into his pocket for later, and then rose carefully.

Morgan trailed him out of the shop to his bike.

"Thank you" she said.

"You're welcome, little sister," he said, his bluff face serious for a moment. "Now, you be careful, and move ye quick, and I'll see you at court by tomorrow."

He started his bike and pulled out into traffic, and Morgan waved as he disappeared into the gloom.

It was only after he was gone into the urban distance that she realized that she did not know where the new official gate would open, and had forgotten to ask.

Morgan threw her cup down into the gutter and stamped on it angrily, and then hurried away.

The Lands That Lie Between

Twenty-Seven
Elsewhere

...The little man ran headlong through the darkness with death on his heels...

Behind him, death ran, hating, howling, hungering for his blood. Four legged shadows, claws and paws and sharp, sharp teeth, loping in concert and in pursuit, commanded to hunt and more than glad to do so.

The hob could hear them pounding the pavement fast behind him, laughing and snarling as they gradually overtook him. He knew they could have caught him at once, but they were playing with him, savoring the excitement before pulling their prey down, reveling in the sound of his panicked breathing and the heart pounding in his tiny chest.

They were enjoying this. A lot.

The thought of what would come at chase's end made him run even faster...

Down the alley...

Around the corner...

Through the hole in the fence...

Maybe he could lose them...

Maybe he could trick them...

Maybe he could reach a more public area-one where they would hesitate to come out into the open and be seen by human kind.

Down the alley, and around the corner, and through the jagged hole in the fence. Step for step and trick for trick, the shadow horde kept horrid pace with him, laughing darkly as they gradually overtook him.

Just another five minutes, five tiny minutes and there were more public places ahead, places where the little man might have a chance.

But he knew that he'd never reach them in time.

Around one more corner.

And, there in the dark and private alley, the shadow pack overtook him,

And took him down hard.

Claws and teeth flashed…

And, in pain and panic, he cried out…

Twenty-Eight
Morgan

Morgan scuttled down the street, eyes flicking nervously from side to side, hyper-alert for any signs of danger. She understood what the motorcyclist had said. He was a very visible target, and she would probably be much safer away from him.

Still, she felt very abandoned and alone...

Setting her shoulders and lifting her head up, she tried her best to think more positively. She was still up and mobile. She'd eluded the forces of Darkness repeatedly so far. She still had her health.

Probably best to get under cover first and figure out what she was going to do next. She wrapped her coat closer around her, turned on her heel and moved quickly away from the open street.

And as she passed the alley, she heard a cry of pain.

Morgan's head snapped around, focusing on the sound. She moved in closer to the corner of the building, and slowly, s–l–o–w–l–y, cautiously peered around the corner's edge...

The Lands That Lie Between

Twenty-Nine
Morgan

The alley was dim and full of violent movement. At first, Morgan couldn't really see what was going on, but, as her eyes adjusted, everything came into focus.

She saw the eyes first, the red and glowing eyes. Large and muscular bodies surging and lunging on four sturdy legs. Growling and snarling and yipping with angry eagerness.

And the teeth – so many teeth.

The alley way was alive with a seething mass of hounds, shaggy and smoky colored and indistinct; snapping and snarling and surging at something huddled beyond them in a niche in a wall at the far end of the alley. They didn't see her peering around the corner yet because they were all so focused on whatever was in that niche, surging and pressing and trying their best to get into it against the pressure of their fellow hounds

Morgan almost withdrew back around the corner, prepared to tiptoe away quietly.

Then she heard it again. The cry of pain; and the sound struck to the heart of her.

For two days now, she'd been on the run, hunted and hounded. For two days she'd been plunged into chaos and fear and uncertainty. She'd lost her normal life. She'd lost her friends. She'd lost all certainty about the world around her; about what was fantasy and what was real. She'd been in worse danger than she'd ever dreamed about.

Now, there was someone trapped in the alley in a worse position than she was. Someone in more trouble and pain and more alone than ever she was. Someone who would probably die if nothing happened to change things.

She was not going to let that happen.

She forgot her fear and uncertainty.

She had had enough.

"Har! You!" she cried out angrily, stepping out fully in front of the open mouth to the alley way.

Half a dozen shaggy heads with red eyes glowing snapped around to look at her intently. A low growl rumbled out of half a dozen massive chests, swelling as the dogs focused more closely on her.

"Get off of him," she shouted angrily, clapping her hands together. "Get out of here, you lousy dogs!"

A few of the hounds turned and slowly began to stalk stiffly toward her, while the remainder continued to struggle to get into the niche in the wall.

"Uh-oh," she thought nervously. "I'm in trouble now." And then she heard the cries again beyond the pack, somewhat weaker now.

"Well, if you're gonna go, go big" she thought, grabbing firmly onto the strap of her duffle bag.

"Har!" she cried again, waving one arm. "All of you get out of here!" She slid the duffle from her shoulder and held it by the strap.

The first dog, more courageous that the rest, crouched and then lunged at her.

She swung the duffle bag at him on the end of its strap. It struck him directly on the nose; and now the hard and rigid items in the bag justified their space. The bag hit the dog like a ton of lumpy, pointy bricks, and the hound yelped loudly and backed quickly away from her.

The hounds to each side growled and withdrew slightly, curving and turning, looking for an opening. Several more slid in behind to fill the gap there.

Morgan took a firmer grip with both hands on the duffle bag strap.

"Har!" she yelled again and waded into the mass of dogs, swinging her bag vigorously from side to side, sweeping through the pack.

Dogs yelped and snarled and backed away from the massive duffle. Some went flying, noses hit and eyes watering. One dog tried to flank her, but was caught in the backswing as the bag flew from one side to the other

Morgan continued to move forward one step after another, clearing dogs as she went. The swinging of the massive bag opened a path before her like the Dead Sea, and she moved through as quickly as she could.

As she moved forwards, the dogs she faced were knocked away or withdrawn to the side. She reached the backs of dogs still focused on the niche. The duffle bag smote like thunder into rangy hind quarters, knocking dogs off their feet and taking them by surprise as it hit them. There was more yelping and snarling as the dogs, one by one, were knocked away until at last, Morgan worked her way through the dogs, and came to the end of the alley.

Huddled there in the shallow niche, was a little man. Not a brownie, but a different creature than she'd seen before.

He was small and somewhat stocky, yet well proportioned, like a stevedore in miniature. His hair was brown, and his skin also, and his ears were ever so slightly pointed. He was dressed in brown and green and grey, simple, sturdy clothes, well suited for hard work.

He was in bad shape. Battered, bruised and bleeding from a half a dozen wounds, he was curled up against the wall in a ball, sheltering himself as best he could from the fangs of the savage hounds. His face was screwed up with fear and pain, and his eyes tight closed against the fate that faced him.

He was painful to look at, and Morgan felt her heart break a little just looking at him. Her muscles tensed and her jaw locked as her anger rose. Morgan pivoted on one leg and stood in front of the little man, crouching slightly to give herself a strong and stable stance. She adjusted her grip and glared at the circling hounds.

"Now you hear me, boys" she snarled herself "and you hear me good! You can be good little dogs, or you can be elsewhere."

The dogs continued to snarl and growl and circle, looking for an opening. Several crouched, preparing to leap. Morgan set her back against the wall over the niche sheltering the little man, tensed her shoulders and got ready for what was coming.

The first dog lunged at her, and a second dog immediately followed suit. Morgan heaved from her shoulders, setting the duffle into furious motion.

"Heel!" she roared, as the duffle bag hit the first hound with tremendous force, knocking him to the side and into the wall with a thunk.

"Down!" she shouted, swinging the bag back to catch the second in the head, knocking him to his knees.

"Play dead!" she snarled, catching a third one in the swing area in front of her and sending him flying, howling with pain.

She continued to flail the duffle bag back and forth in front of her, faster and faster, forming an area of impact where no hound could pass without risking pain or serious injury.

The hounds kept coming. They howled and snarled; they lunged and leapt; but not a one of them could pass the whirling field of pain she'd created in front of her, and at last they backed away, still snarling, before turning to run.

"And don't stay!" she called after them, bag brandished furiously.

She waited briefly, in case this was a ruse with hounds creeping back through the shadows. Once it was clear they were not coming back immediately, she turned and knelt down by the little man behind her.

She gently touched his shoulder. He flinched for a moment, and she pulled back her hand.

"Hey. You there. Are you ok?" she said softly to him.

There was a long pause until the little man opened his eyes and blinked at her in the dimness of the alley. His face was pale and his green eyes wide. He looked at her blankly for a moment, and then awareness drained back into his face. He sat bolt upright and started to look about him quickly, looking for any signs of danger.

"They're gone," she soothed, though she wasn't as sure of this as she sounded. "Things are ok. The dogs are gone. Now, are you ok? Are you badly hurt? Do we need to get you to a doctor or a hospital to get fixed up?"

The little man stared at her for a moment, still in shock, as if he couldn't figure out who she was or what she was doing there. Gradually, a timid smile appeared on his face.

"Thank you, no, mum," he said hesitantly "Ain't no hospitals fit for the likes of a hob like me, milady. I'll just bind up these bites then and go about my business, I shall, and I'll be healing with time, I will. But are you yourself all right, mi lady? Did any of those blaggarts lay a tooth to you then or harm you in any other way?"

Adrenalin dropping off for the moment, Morgan stopped and took a brief inventory of herself. While sore and bruised and rather fatigued, she didn't seem to have any serious injuries.

"I seem to be ok," she said.

A horn sounded in the distance. Not a car horn, but rather the kind of horn you hear at the start of a hunt. In the distance, but not that far in the distance.

A look of alarm came into the little man's eyes once more. "Best we both be off then!" he shouted, leaping to his feet. "I've already had a taste of the hospitality in these parts, and I'll be thinking that neither you nor I, milady, will have a taste for more."

He seized her by the hand and drew her to her feet from where she had knelt beside him, and then they were running like the wind towards the open end of the alley.

The horn sounded again, and their feet grew wings. Out of the alley and into the street and running away from the sound of the horn and hounds gathering once more in the distance.

"In here!" she shouted and broke left, dragging him behind her through a door. The shop she'd pulled him into was full of soaps, shampoos and lotions, all redolent with powerful scents.

She dashed towards the back exit, cornering sharply so the attendant missed her and her companion with the perfume sample but liberally scented the air behind them.

"That should confuse their little doggy noses" she thought spitefully, as they burst out of the entrance into the mall.

They broke left and dropped into a brisk walk, both heads swiveling from side to side watching for any sign of danger.

"Where next?" he asked, a frightened look in his eyes.

"Don't know, don't know" she said, settling her duffel on her shoulder. "I'm making it up as I go along."

They kept walking briskly past shop after shop, looking for shelter, for anyway out. Something caught Morgan's eye further down the mall, and she paused, stepping aside into an alcove and drawing her small companion with her.

With her right eye open, she saw a tall blonde woman tanned and toned, with a toddler on a baby harness rambling in front of her. With her left eye, on the other hand, the blond became a tall cowled figure, with a massive hound pulling at the lead.

The small man turned and followed her eye. "Quick" he hissed, and darted across the central aisle, moving closer to an exit. She tried to follow, but her movement was more visible than her companion's. The hunter's head turned in her direction.

She looked across at where the little man huddled in a doorway. There was no way that she could take cover there now- but she could still draw the hunter away. She nodded slightly and then turned on her heel and went in the other direction.

Reflected in the storefront windows, she could see the hunter begin to speed up, orienting in on her movement. She picked up the pace on her power walk, and noticed the hunter speeded up as well. Hunter and dog swept past the little man's hiding place, and she had a brief moment of satisfaction before she had to concentrate on what she was going to do now. Up ahead she could see the center hub of the mall, with its benches and plants and the great glass elevator.

The elevator! That would do.

Putting on a burst of speed, she dashed forwards. People were offloading from the elevator and she had to fight her way through the crowds disembarking as she got closer, slowing her. She couldn't see them now, but she could almost feel the hunter and his dog gaining on her.

The elevator was filling, filling, and for one bad moment, Morgan thought that the space was gone for this load.

"Just one more!" she squeaked in a perky voice that didn't match the feeling in the pit of her stomach. She slid in sideways and turned, plastering herself across the front of the elevator, before reaching out to push the button.

The doors to the elevator crept slowly closed. Morgan had never seen two doors close more slowly as, in between them, she watched the mastiff come barreling towards her, teeth bared. Closer... closer... and then the doors snapped shut just short of its nose.

"Did you see that crazy baby?" one teenager said to

his buddy directly behind her. "Wonder who let him off his leash?"

Morgan took a deep breath and relaxed a bit, as the elevator climbed upwards. Looking over her shoulder through the glass elevator walls, she could just see her erstwhile companion, as he skittered out of the mall door, around a corner and out of sight.

"Well, at least there's that," she thought to herself, and, feeling slightly cocky for a moment, waved cheerfully at the hunter as she got off on the third floor and lost herself in the crowds again.

The Lands That Lie Between

Thirty
Morgan

An hour later, she was not feeling so cocky.

While she'd continued to elude the eleven hunters, she had realized she still didn't know where and when the gate would open next and hadn't gotten a chance to ask before she and the little man had parted ways.

Given that the only other people she could think of who might know were currently trying to capture or kill her, this left her kind of stuck.

She was standing in line for coffee in the food court at a point which gave her a magnificent viewpoint of any approaching trouble. Moving up in line, she reached in her pocket for change, and instead pulled out a business card.

The tarot reader. He'd seemed to know a bit about what was happening to her now. Maybe he'd know where she could find the gate.

She dropped out of line and moved to a nearby table. Dialing the phone number on the card, she got a cheerful female voice informing her that the people at this number could be found at the renaissance faire this weekend-drop by or leave a message at the beep.

She felt like crying. Every door seemed to be slamming in her face and time was running out.

"Wait a minute" she thought, pulling herself together. "The renaissance faire. Maybe I could reach him directly there." Nerves stretching, Morgan did a quick search online. The website for the faire said the faire would be running into the evening tonight, and listed an address, as well as the information that the faire could be reached on the local bus system.

Looking out the window, she could see a bus stop just outside.

Carefully, Morgan began to make her way down and out of the mall.

Thirty-One
Elsewhere

The weather was damp and raw, fit mostly for huddling into your collar and looking for gloves that should be lurking in your pockets. The air was full of music from the bar down the street.

A buxom goth girl was walking to her car four blocks away. She had a confident walk, a pentacle around her neck, and a really striking outfit on. She also had her keys out, and, on her attractive face, a scowl that could strip paint.

"When will these guys get a clue that "no" means "no"?" she thought crankily. "I really hated to knock that one out. When will I meet a guy that understands personal space? Is there even such a guy on the face of the planet?"

A sound came from the alley beyond her. Her head whipped about, and her body followed, settling into a comfortably familiar fighting stance, keys brandished as improvised brass knuckles.

"He didn't flank me, did he?" she thought crossly. "Not in the mood to kick his butt a second time, but also not in the mood for any one messing with me."

"Come on," she said loudly. "I don't want trouble, but if you do, you've certainly found it."

She bent her knees slightly and tensed, preparing for the initial rush of a drunken brawl or a criminal attack.

. . . . Neither of which came. . . .

She waited.

After a minute, she said "Um, if you're planning something, I'd really like to get on with it. I've got classes tomorrow and still have homework, so I really need to get home…"

Still nothing.

After a few minutes, her tension eased slightly, and she dropped into a less aggressive but alert stance. Slowly, carefully, she crept forwards and leaned to peer around the edge of the alley.

The light was dim in the alley, but still enough to see there was no one there, and no possible place for anyone to hide. Straightening, she grinned and shook her head at how skittish she was. Turning, she started to walk away.

And then she heard a noise behind her in the alley. A faint noise-almost faint enough to be her imagination-but not quite.

Spinning, she dropped into ready stance again.

"Hell-o…" she said, moving forwards into the alley. "Just about sick of this…"

She jumped as she heard a faint moan at her feet in a pile of rubble too small for any human to hide in. She took a deep breath, and then bent down carefully; ready to jump back quickly if something tried to eat her face…

Like a rat…

Or an alien from another planet…

Or a killer doll…

Or a rat. Definitely…if…a…rat…

She shuddered a bit. Not much threw her, but having her face eaten was high on the list.

Looking into a tunnel of intermeshed rubble, she peered into the darkness. A set of deep golden eyes peered back at her from the depths of the tunnel.

"Mew!" echoed out of the rubble.

Not a rat, then.

Unless it was a bilingual rat...

"Kitty?" she said tentatively. "Here, kitty kitty. Are you all right in there? Are you hurt?"

She heard another weak and plaintive mew. Looking down, she saw a trail of blood leading into the tunnel.

"Oh my. That doesn't look good." she said, her heart melting as it always when confronted with something small and furry in trouble. "Hang tight, kitty. Momma's coming!"

She took off her new leather jacket and dropped it on the filthy ground without another thought. Best to protect herself from broken glass and give herself a safe place to lie on while she excavated the frightened cat from his refuge. Kneeling down smoothly and then lying at full length upon her stomach, she crawled cautiously into the claustrophobic space inside the trash, inch by inch, making soothing noises as she went to keep from alarming the cat.

In the next few minutes, she touched a number of unpleasant things she'd rather not think about, but then she felt crusted fur shift under her fingertips. The cat moved gingerly, backing painfully away from her.

"No, no, kitty. I'm here to help you." she cooed, hoping desperately to calm him enough to keep him in reach. "Goddess, mother!' she muttered under her breath "will you stay still? I'm just trying to get you out so I can get you the help you need."

The cat tensed for a moment. Then, wonder of wonders, he relaxed and lay still, letting her get her hands around him. He winced once and hissed when she closed her grasp on him. She tensed and waited for the inevitable panic and clawing attack that came with rescuing an injured cat. Surprisingly enough, it didn't come. The cat twitched at her touch repeatedly, but relaxed into her grasp and let her pull him from the wreckage.

Inch by inch, she wiggled backwards, sheltering the cat as much as possible, until the pair of them were out of the rubbish. She held him closely, and he melted into her.

Picking up her coat, she carried the cat down to the street where she could see him better in the sunlight.

She gasped. The cat had once been an attractive, golden tabby, but was now a mass of gaping wounds and burns on every part of his body. He was still bleeding, but most of the wounds were partially closed, and his body tensed with pain. This cat had been terribly injured in the last few hours, but had somehow managed to break away from his attackers and crawled into the garbage to hide.

Despite all of this, he summoned up the strength to purr at her.

"Oh, baby." she said. "Who did this awful thing to you? You're in really bad shape. Let's get you wrapped up here, and then I'll take you to someone who can really help."

Stepping back into the shelter of the alley, she stripped off her shirt to wrap the cat in to protect it, and threw the coat back on over her underwear. Quickly picking up the cat, she walked as fast as she could without jostling her patient towards her car four blocks away.

"Hold on there, kitty," she said. "Momma's gonna get you to a healer. She'll know what to do for you."

She reached her car, wrenched open the door, and carefully loaded her passenger into the back. She threw herself bodily into the driver's seat, and peeled out, heading for an alternative healer she knew to be extremely effective in cases where lesser medics failed. Many times she'd watched the energy flowing from this healer's hands close wounds, reverse seemingly unstoppable conditions, and bring peace and freedom from pain to people and animals in extreme distress.

She only hoped that she would be in time.

"Goddess Mother," she prayed as she drove "please bless that fellow in the back seat, and watch over him. Help me get him to our destination safely and alive. Bless the healer's hands and spirit, and help her to help him…"

In the back of the car, Sam closed his eyes and passed out…

The Lands That Lie Between

Thirty-Two
Morgan

It was mid afternoon by the time that the bus pulled up at the gates to the renaissance faire. Morgan waited cautiously while other passengers got off, looking carefully out of the bus windows for any sign of pursuit.

She'd felt so scared and vulnerable since she'd lost Sam. She didn't know where to go, and there was danger everywhere she went. She missed Sam's guidance, but more than that, she missed Sam himself, both the wise and wise-cracking guardian and the cat who had been with her for as long as she could remember.

She'd never felt so alone.

Her eyes dampened for a moment; and then she set her shoulders and raised her head. She couldn't do anything about her lost companion now, but she might be able to get some guidance here at least. The tarot reader's schedule had said that he and his lady would be working here today.

Morgan took one last look around, and slipped quietly from the bus. She bought a ticket and stepped into another world.

The faire was crammed full with sound and color and good times happening. A maze of booths before her, filled with exotic food, homespun crafts and amazing experiences. Visiting Klingons rubbed shoulders with exalted lords and ladies, guys in baseball caps stood in line with barbarian warriors, and little children with painted faces danced with buxom women in bodices and energetic men in bells.

And there were elves…

Morgan froze, and then relaxed again. The trio of elves ahead was only teenagers in pointy ears and splendid costumes. She grinned weakly, and then moved forward, looking for the reader she sought.

It was overwhelming. Everything lately was overwhelming; and she wasn't sure if she had enough strength left to find the man she was looking for.

"Pardon me, milady," said a cheerful voice at her elbow. "You look a bit at sea there. May I help?"

Looking down, Morgan saw a short, round woman in a blue gown. Her long brown hair was tucked up beneath a circlet and veil; and her face was intelligent and kind.

"Yes" said Morgan. "I'm looking for a tarot card reader who's working here today, but I didn't expect all this..." she said, throwing up her hands.

"First time at faire, eh?" nodded the woman. "It can be a bit of a leap. I'll see you straight though. What's this reader look like?"

"He's tall, with long silvered hair and a mustache and a beard..." began Morgan.

"...And he looks like Santa Claus, the biker years?" said the woman, laughing. "Bless you, that's convenient. That's my husband, and I was heading back to the booth anyway. Come with me, dear."

Morgan found herself trailing after the woman, like a duckling after a mother duck. Her guide threaded through the crowded lanes and twisting paths with ease and grace, and Morgan had a hard time keeping up with her at points. She chattered as she went; here calling a greeting to a merchant woman, there pointing out a shop that sold the most delicious hand-squeezed limeade, until Morgan wondered if there was anyone here this woman was not familiar with.

"So, how did you meet my husband?" the woman asked pleasantly as she walked.

"He did my first tarot reading earlier this week at a shop in my neighborhood. It said some dramatic things, and I wasn't sure what I thought about it at the time, since then, though, it's all been coming true. Things have happened that I never could have imagined."

"I've lost my guide and my way, and I keep finding myself in danger. Your husband said if I needed advice or help, I could come to you. So, here I am," said Morgan, holding back tears. "I don't know what else to do."

The woman stopped and looked her straight in the face. "So you're the one with the quest," she said. "He said you might show up. We'd best get you under wraps as soon as we can."

Her eyes strayed over Morgan's shoulder and locked on something behind her. "Or maybe even sooner," she said excessively casually. "Come this way, milady. Quickly, quietly, and don't look back, now."

She pivoted and dove between two vendor's booths. Morgan turned and caught a glimpse of a magic glow further down the lane.

Sidhe. Real sidhe, not happy visitors playing elven dress-up. Armed to the teeth, searching the faire, and blending in naturally with the fantasy fun and quirky ambience. Here was one place where they wouldn't have to try too hard to conceal their presence.

Morgan gulped, and dove between the tents, after her guide. The woman scurried between the backs of tents, moving quietly but quickly and picking up speed as she went. As she passed, occasionally a startled vendor would peer out the back of a tent, but a wave and a finger to her lips, and no overt signs of her passage were visible from the public part of the faire.

She looked back and gestured to Morgan, urging her to be quiet but catch up. Morgan was more than glad to, although she couldn't move as quickly through the maze as her leader.

The sidhe! She'd thought she'd lost them. How had they found her here? More to the point, how was she going to escape them? She couldn't play hide and seek forever, and she hadn't seen a single good stronghold here where she could lock them out or long-term hiding place.

Ahead, her guide slowed. "Almost there" she muttered quietly. "We don't have much leeway. When we get to our booth, stay very quiet, go along with what I tell you, and don't lose your nerve. Just know that himself and I will take good care of you, and that, if things get sticky, we've lots of friends to call on in the neighborhood."

Morgan nodded, eyes large.

The woman stopped in back of a pop-up that looked like every other tent at the faire. She listened for a moment, then turned back to Morgan.

"Here we go," she said.

Lips close to the back wall, she whispered "Dear, I'm coming in and I've got that new friend of yours with me-the one you wanted me to meet. There are people here looking for her she'd just as soon not see, so I think we're going to have to dance quickly here."

"Ready to go" came the voice of the tarot reader. "I

could feel you coming across the camp."

"If you could, chances are they could too." The woman said. "Could you perhaps power up a bit, and make things a bit more challenging for them?"

The woman turned and whispered in Morgan's ear. "Not a lot of good places to hide you onsite where they won't find you sooner or later, so we'll have to hide you in plain sight. In our tent, there's a pile of duffle sitting on the ground between us, covered by a Celtic bedspread and mostly concealed by our tables. When I count down to one, I'll pull up the back wall and the bedspread together. I want you to slide in on top of the equipment, while I lower the bedspread back over you. We'll put a couple of light things on top of you, and misdirect anyone who comes hunting until we can give you the help you need and I figure out how to get you safely away again."

"But, won't they find me out in the open like that?" said Morgan.

"Visually, you'll be hidden. If they're tracking you by magick or your energy field, our tent is one of the best places you could be, because our personal energy fields, should mask yours from them. If they're tracking by smell, my husband's pipe should befuddle them a bit. We know a thing or two about confusing a tracker."

"Honey, if they come for you, we'll trick them; and if we can't trick them, we'll magick them; and if we can't magick them, we'll fight them; and we've got lots and lots of help in these parts. You'll be fine here with us."

"Besides, I believe you came here looking for information and help. It'd be a shame if you didn't get either. Now, are you ready?"

Morgan nodded, her heart in her throat.

The woman counted down silently with her fingers. Three. Two. One.

At one, she stooped and caught up tent wall and edge of bedspread together, making a close little nest for Morgan to crawl into. Morgan slipped quickly into place on top of the mound of luggage. The table cloth dropped down, covering her, as her guide stepped into the tent. A cloak was laid over the pile, providing extra coverage for most of Morgan but leaving a small area free at her face.

The table cloth was opaque but thin. While Morgan was concealed beneath it (especially with the extra layer of cloak), she could easily breathe through it, and, more importantly, dimly see what was happening around her. When she closed her right eye, she saw a faint golden glow that seemed to fill the tent. She could see the crowds in the lane in front of the tent. She could see the tarot reader loosening his sword slightly in its scabbard.

And she could see the three sidhe hunters coming down the lane.

Morgan stiffened with fear. "They're coming," she said tensely. "They'll find me."

The tarot reader casually rested his elbow on the pile in a way that wouldn't let her bolt.

"No, they won't. You just watch my lady work," he said proudly, puffing on a corncob pipe full of some eccentric mixture.

The lady closed her eyes and concentrated for a moment. The golden light filling the tent grew stronger and brighter. She opened her eyes, smiled broadly, took a deep breath and began to call out in a sing-song manner, like a

Gregorian chant.

"Palmistry! Tarot! Crystal Dowsing! I Ching! We see all; we know all; we tell much! Cards turned! Coins tossed! Palms read and futures told!" She cried their wares, and the sound of her voice echoed down the lane and across the faire grounds.

"Palmistry!..Tarot!.."This time her husband joined in, his pleasant tenor blending perfectly with her pert supralto.

The sidhe hunters stalked down the lane, peering ferociously into each tent in turn, looking for their quarry. Morgan tensed in hiding as they approached.

Suddenly, the woman's face became coy and cloying. She beamed and made inescapable eye contact with each hunter in turn, shifting back and forth rapidly between each of them, so none could escape. She winked. She preened. She fluttered her eyelashes. She flirted with a heavy hand, to a level approaching (but not quite reaching) parody.

"Why, good day, my handsome young lords." she purred in a voice of equal parts honey and cream. "Art thou having an enjoyable day at the faire today? Might I offer thee palmistry..? Tarot..? I Ching...? Over eighty years of cumulative experience at your service. How may we serve you...?"

One hunter growled "We've no time for such foolishness. We have a quest to complete before the day is done."

"A quest!" she exclaimed, riding over the top of his petulance. "What could be finer? And what could be more helpful on a quest than knowledge, knowledge from sources mysterious and arcane? Come in! Come in!"

"He is right. We have no time..." started a second hunter looking a bit alarmed.

"No time?" she cooed. "But an accurate reading will save you hours of time and make your lives much easier. Come in!" She leapt up and ran around the table to draw a chair back invitingly.

The sidhe were beginning to look alarmed. "We've really got to go. Sorry..." said the third hunter, as the three of them backed away rapidly.

"And there they go." said the woman, no longer in clinging vine mode. "It's always the self important ones who are intimidated and embarrassed so easily. If they had a decent sense of self, they'd just laugh at my nonsense and enjoy it, but the pompous ones are always so shy and vulnerable underneath. Speaking of underneath, are you all right under there?"

The Celtic tablecloth vibrated slightly. Morgan was shoving her fist into her mouth to keep from laughing out loud, and almost choking in the process. It was the first laugh she'd had in a while, and it felt very good.

"Oh, I'm fine, just fine." She snorted. "This luggage is a bit lumpy to lie on, and I think my leg will go to sleep if I stay like this for long, but compared with fleeing for my life from elven assassins, this is sheer Heaven."

The tarot reader relaxed slightly as he watched the unseelie hunters hurriedly move off down the medieval lane...

Thirty-Three
Morgan

The tarot reader relaxed slightly as he watched the Unseelie hunters hurriedly move off down the medieval lane. He took his hand off the hilt of his Celtic short sword.

"What brings you to this neck of the woods, other than the obvious?" he asked mildly out of the side of his mouth. "Can't imagine you're here just to hide in our luggage."

Morgan returned to her situation with a jolt.

"It's a long story," she said quietly "but there's just not enough time to go over it all. The short version is that your reading was accurate."

"Yesterday, I thought you were just telling me a pretty story to amuse me about elves, and quests, and magic loose in the world we live in. I've found out I was wrong about that–big time wrong. Within the last twenty four hours, magick has reared up out of nowhere and hit me square in the face, I'm on the run from elvish assassins, I've been drawn into some kind of life or death adventure, and my mundane life is gone forever, as far as I can see.

"It seems I have elven blood and I'm distantly related to the current King, who's on his deathbed. Evidently I need to get to the elven court because I'm part of the process to determine the new king. I set out for the court with my friend Sam, but there are a lot of other folks who'd like to eliminate the competition. We were waylaid, Sam is hurt or dead, and I'm out here wandering around on my own."

"I don't know where Sam is; and if he's even alive

or not. I don't know where I'm going. I don't know how I'm going to get there without being killed myself, and you were the only other option that I could think of…"

There was a brief silence, while the two psychics looked at each other. "Well, that's certainly a lot for you to deal with all at once, but I think that we can help you a bit with that," the tarot reader said softly. "Let's see."

He reached into a leather pouch and drew out a pack of use-worn tarot cards. Pausing a moment, he closed his eyes and concentrated before beginning to shuffle.

Under the tablecloth, Morgan shifted slightly, easing her weight away from something poking up into her hip. Looking up through the cloth, she saw the tarot reader lift the card on the top of the deck and stare at it intently.

"I'll look for information that could be useful to you." said the bearded man, laying down the first card and peering at the second one. "Lets start with where the gates to the elven court will open up next, and when. They're not always open and they move about, you know."

"Dear" he said, turning to his lady "while I'm sorting out directions, can you figure out how we're going to get her past all of those hunters and away from here?"

"As good as done," said his wife.

"First of all, your friend, Sam, is alive," said the tarot reader, moving on to a third card and pulling a map from a bag on his chair. "By the way, you didn't mention that he was a talking cat."

"He's alive?" she whispered. "Sam's alive? Is he all right? Where is he? Is there any way I can get to him?"

"He's actually with someone we know." The tarot reader said "and not out of the story of your life yet-not by a long shot. I'm seeing the two of you will definitely be re-united and that you have a lot further to go together in life. That means we definitely have to get you safely out of here and on to where you can meet up again."

"The faire is full of unseelie hunters, and more of them are being drawn in all the time by all of the Light they're sensing here." added his lady, looking up from a metal mirror she was gazing into. "The faster we get you out of here, the easier it'll be for you to slip through the net they're casting for any bearers of the Light. We'd best act quickly, to give you your best shot at escaping and connecting up with your friend again."

"Fortunately, I've a few ideas on that." She added.

"Of course you do," said the tarot reader, smiling deep in his beard. "You always have some idea or other for whatever situation we're in."

He stared again at the card in his hand and then laid it down on the table, drawing three more cards. Reaching into a pouch and pulling out a pen, he unfolded the map and started marking it, still looking at the cards fanned out on the table in front of him.

"The cards tell me you've already received help along the way" he told Morgan as he wrote "and that you'll continue to receive help, often from unexpected sources and when least expected. You'll be helped upon your quest by others, but, because many of the people who will come to help you are carriers of the Light themselves and therefore targets for the Unseelie, these people may need to help you and then move quickly away from you again to keep from drawing more trouble down on you and your quest. There will yet be times when you'll walk alone, or with only your cat at your side, and you'll have to be strong and wise and brave at those times. Even if you don't really feel that way."

A chill ran down Morgan's spine as she huddled under the Celtic cloth. Her position now was lumpy, uncomfortable and undignified, but she hadn't felt this safe for the last two days, and the thought of leaving this awkward refuge and heading back out into the sidhe infested world terrified her.

A hand gently touched her shoulder, and Morgan almost shrieked before she turned her head and saw it was the short, round lady.

"Don't be afraid, my dear," the palmist said softly. "Never let the truth frighten you. My husband gives very good advice, but it's sometimes more than people are ready for all at once."

"Unfortunately" she said "you don't really have time to ease into it. You have fallen into a heroic story, and that can feel like a bumpy road at first; but you must remember there's a reason that you're here in the midst of it, and a providence that guides your steps; a reason why it's you and not someone else."

"The story of the hero always begins with someone ordinary, someone like you or me. They're always ordinary until they encounter extraordinary events. The hero is that person who becomes extraordinary in response to extraordinary situations."

"But those are just stories." whispered Morgan.

"There's a reason stories are like that." The palmist said. "We tell tales of heroes, because those stories teach us the truth – that there's a hero inside of each of us, and that it's up to us whether we become that hero or not."

"These are extraordinary circumstances." The woman said. "and you have a heroine inside of you. The question is will you let that hero out..?"

Morgan thought a moment. Would she let that hero out..? She didn't know if she could let that hero out into the world; but she did know that she couldn't spend her life hiding under a blanket on a lumpy pile of luggage. She'd just have to do the best that she could, and hope that that was enough. Hope that she was the hero of her own story, and not just the collateral damage...

Morgan took a deep breath, and then another; and she felt her fear lessen. She felt surprisingly calmer, given the danger ahead and her current ridiculous position. She shifted her position slightly again, checking for cramped muscles and easing them so they wouldn't fail her if she had to move quickly.

Beside her, the palmist waved at someone passing in the lane outside of the tent. "Dear!" she called "could I possibly borrow you for just a moment?"

Peeking through the bedspread, Morgan saw a dark stocky man with a pentacle, an extravagant mustache, an air of competence, and turn towards them.

"Why certainly, my lady!" he said, smiling warmly as he hurried into the tent.

"I've a bit of a *special* situation going on now." She said. "Do you understand what I'm saying?"

His hand went to the pentacle for a moment. "I believe that I do, my lady." He said.

"It's not how we usually do things but we've a lady hiding under the bedspread at my elbow here. She's hiding because there are some rather *special* people looking for her-looking rather hard if truth be told; and it will be a very bad thing if they find her."

"Now, I know you like helping damsels in distress. We're going to help her escape, and I was hoping you and your merry band could help us do that."

He grinned fiercely at her. "It would be my great pleasure, my lady. What can I and my fellows do to be of service to your fine selves and the lady here?"

She took his shoulder, leaning him cautiously out of the tent. "Do you see those dashing fellows down the lane with the pointed ears?' she said quietly.

He nodded briskly. "There's a bit of a glow on those boys." He noted.

"That's because they're the real deal, and they mean business. Now I don't know what they'll do or how aggressive they may get, whether physically or in some special way. Just tell your friends not to confront them directly or put themselves in harm's way in any manner. Just distract them a bit."

"We can certainly do that," he grinned. "I know some of the most distracting people around. Does your friend need transport as well? I've got someone who can break away long enough to take her to her next stop, though he must be back within the hour."

"That would be very nice," smiled the woman. "I'm sure our guest would appreciate any help you can give her."

He took the palmist's hand, bending low to kiss it; and as he did, he gently touched the bedspread beside her. "Have no fear, my lady" he said quietly. "We'll get you safely out of here."

144

He stood up and, smiling broadly, left the tent. Morgan could hear him greeting friends as he moved down the lane. She wasn't sure exactly why, but suddenly she felt more at ease.

"Well, that's done, and well done indeed," said the woman, smiling "We can definitely count on him and his very distracting friends. Now that there's a diversion under way, the next stage is to figure out just how to get you safely out of here. And, you know, I think that I might just have an idea on that."

She got up and stuck her head out of the back of the tent. Morgan could hear her talking quietly to someone.

"That's good timing" said the tarot reader. He stuck the map he'd gotten from his wife under the edge of the bedspread into Morgan's hand. "I've noted the next three locations for the entrance to the Gentry court. I've also jotted down some notes on things you may need to know to get in, such as when the gate opens at various places.

"We can't go with you on your journey. Under certain conditions, we'd make you far more noticeable, and that would offset the advantages you might have by having us near you. We can have a driver take you out to where your friend, Sam, is recovering, so you'll have him to support you on your journey. And you can reach us by phone or email, if you need more help or support. If you need help, please do call. Even if we're not in your area, there may be something we can do to help. Now, if I'm not mistaken, I believe I hear my lovely wife coming back again, presumably with some kind of cunning plan to whisk you away, if I know her."

The back wall of the tent flipped up, and the woman

came bustling through it. "I think I've got things set up so we can get you out of the Faire safely," she said quietly. "In a minute, the distraction should start. When I say "go", I want you to slide out the back of the tent, same as you came in, and follow me. Be sure to follow my lead. I'm going to walk you out of the Faire and see you safely transported away."

"Dear" she said to her husband "I'll hide her energy by putting her inside of my own. I'd like you to boost your own field as well, so there are more things for the hunters to investigate or follow. I'd also like you to watch our back trail, and throw some lovely obstacles in their path if they happen to latch onto us; and don't you get hurt being protective and brave. You know I love you and I want you around for a long, long time."

She bent and kissed him for emphasis.

He held her tightly a moment more than necessary. "Be careful too, my love. I've become attached to you."

She laughed. "Don't worry about me. They won't lay a finger on me." She turned back to where Morgan was hidden under the tablecloth.

"Now, my lady- has my husband given you directions to get where you need to go? Is there anything else you need of us? You may electronically be able to reach us later on, but there are some things better in person. Now's the best time to ask."

"When I got my tarot reading, your husband asked me if there was anything I didn't understand or needed explained," said Morgan. "I didn't have questions then, but I sure have them now. Will I get where I'm going? What do I need to do to succeed in my quest? How do I bring about a happy ending to this nightmare fairy tale I find myself in?"

"Good questions, all three," the tarot reader said. "Dear, I think this is more in your line of work. Will you?"

"Certainly." said the woman. "Happy endings are right up my line and my very favorite things of all. Take my hand, my dear." She said, sliding it gently under the bedspread. Morgan grasped her hand firmly, and felt a warm tingle coming from it. It felt to Morgan like the air around her became warmer, and the gentle golden glow that filled the tent grew brighter.

"Will you arrive?" said the woman. "If you follow your instincts, you will, and you will in good time."

"What do you need to succeed? Your courage, your wits and the friends that you make along the way. The gifts that you receive and the gifts of your own heart and soul are all that you need to triumph."

"And how do you bring about the happy ending? Be brave. Use what you have in a way no one thought of. And trust your heart, for it tells you what you truly need to know. Does that give you what you need?"

Morgan was silent for a moment, and then grinned crookedly. "I think so. It'll do. It'll have to. From what you say, we're on a pretty tight schedule here."

The woman laughed with her. "That's the spirit. The answers would make more sense if you had time to sit and let them sink in. Unfortunately, time is in deplorably short supply right now. I'd say keep these things in mind and watch for signs of them on the way. When you've finished your quest, come back and see me, and I'll give you a full reading, with time to mull things over, ask for clarification, and really get the full worth of us. On the house."

The breath caught in Morgan's throat. "You're saying I'm going to survive this?"

The woman laughed kindly again, and picked up her cloak. "You surely will if I've anything to say about it; and I certainly do. Now look sharp, dear-it's time to go."

Thirty-Four
Morgan

It was time to get moving.

The palmist stood, turned and caught up bedspread and back wall of tent together in one polished motion. Morgan slid quickly out in the same way she'd gone in, and the woman dropped both bedspread and wall, smoothly masking her departure.

Morgan's guide took two steps to the back wall across the alley and hissed gently, pausing and listening before sticking her head briefly into the tent.

"They're ready for us" she said. "Come in, dear, and keep quiet."

Morgan followed her into a large pavilion, with the front flaps closed. Racks of cloaks, gowns, tunics and hose surrounded her, with shelves displaying silver circlets and custom clasps. There was a group of women waiting in the tent-women who looked curious but kind.

"Hello, ladies." said the tarot reader's wife. "As you may have heard, my friend here is being stalked by some very *special* people, and I need your help in getting her out of here safely. We're going to play "button, button, who's got the button?" Anyone want to help?"

"Sounds like fun," said the willowy blonde in the front. "What do we do?"

"I want everyone in pairs with an energy worker per pair." the palmist said. "I want cloaks on, hoods up, so they can't tell us apart easily by sight. I'd like you to spread out and crank up your auras, so the hunters are confused. Most of all, I want you to all play it safe. These guys are dangerous, physically and metaphysically, and I don't want anyone confronting them and getting hurt. Just turn up the energy, spread out, and make it as hard for them to catch up with us as possible."

"This we can do." said a dark haired woman with a pentacle. She closed her eyes and started murmuring to herself, and several of her fellows followed suit. As they chanted, Morgan felt the air around her warming, and feeling almost bubbly. Closing her right eye, she saw the air was full of colors, blue and green and the gold of her guide, amongst others.

Morgan's guide looked at the clothing merchant, who nodded and passed her a cloak of grey wool. "You'll wear my cloak." the palmist said to Morgan "and I'll borrow this one. Now all we need to do is wait for the sound of a party breaking loose."

And then, pandemonium. Down the front street, came the drumming of drums, and the droning of pipes, clapping and cheering and catcalls and the sound of a really good time spontaneously coming into being.

"That's our cue." said the palmist, pulling back the tent flap. Hoods up and faces shaded, pairs of women flooded from the tent, chattering about fittings and bidding each other good day, as they separated in all directions.
Morgan saw a sign that said "Closed for Wedding Fittings – reopening in 15 minutes" in front of the tent as they turned down the path.

"Stick close to me."Morgan's guide said. "Let's walk arm in arm, shall we? If they're tracking by energy, my aura should mask yours, and if hunting by scent, the mustard soup I had for lunch should give them a problem too. Besides, with all those mysterious women going every which way, they should have a hard time finding you. Hood up, confident walk, act like you own the faire, my dear."

Morgan stuck close to her guide, hardly believing this would work. A quick glance down the street revealed her pursuers caught firmly in the midst of a seething mass of belly dancers, bagpipe players, pirates, crowned heads, handsome rascals, pretend elves, villains, and one guy in a dragon suit, all engaging in their own brand of amusement as vigorously as possible. Try as they might to reach the edge of this joyous mass of reality, time and again, the hunters found their passage blocked by one more piece of street theater, one more extravagant flirtation, one more deed of daring do, one more exotic shimmy, one more bit of life that somehow would not let them pass.

Morgan giggled, and drew her hood even further forward to hide her grin. She could almost hear their blood pressure rising from where she stood.

Hood forward, her guide threw her arm around her shoulder and they walked on companionably. They were just two women in deep conversation.

"Keep close to me," she muttered quietly. "We want your trail muddled by mine as much as possible. I'm going to take you around some side streets, to keep you out of view as much as possible, and, if needed, I'll take you by the back ways to conceal you. Hopefully, I've made things so confusing that they won't be able to pick you out of the background. I tend to be good at confusing folks, if I do say so myself."

They sauntered through the faire, keeping mostly to side streets and alleys, stepping into shops when hunters passed, and making themselves blend in with every other visitor at the faire. As they walked, Morgan's guide carefully passed a small pouch to her.

"Keep that safe." she said. "There are nails in there. Cold iron nails. Cold iron can damage many of the Sidhe, and they don't like that. Keep in mind though, that tolerances vary. It's painful to some, and death to others, and it's not always easy to tell which are which. You might just make one angry as opposed to stopping him cold, so you don't want to use it unless you have no other choice."

"When it comes to the sidhe," muttered the woman quietly out of the side of her mouth "it's always better to trick them than to meet them head on."

As they came up towards the gate, the woman suddenly clutched at Morgan's sleeve, turning her and marching her towards the lady's room behind them. She put her head in the door and looked around, then pulled Morgan in after her as quickly as possible.

"Drat! There's one of the rascals at the gate." She said. "I'm going to have to come up with something else." She reached down into a pocket in her sleeve, pulled out a cell phone and dialed like mad.

"Hello. It's me," she said. "Is your driver outside the gates? Good job, man. We're pinned down in the lady's facilities-there's one more of them watching the gate. I'm going to have to figure out a way to get her past him, and when we come out, we may be coming fast. Your driver should be very near the gate and ready to roll. A dark blue van with a purple dragon's head bobber on the aerial? I think that we can spot that. Good bye."

Shutting down the phone, she turned to Morgan.

"Now we need another cunning plan. Give me a minute-I'm sure that I've got another somewhere about my person," she said, her brow furrowed.

Suddenly, she looked at her watch. "I've got it!" she said with satisfaction, dialing furiously on her phone again.

"Dear, we're pinned down in the lady's side of the Royal Flush," she said rapidly. "There's another one of the buggers at the gate, watching all traffic in and out. Don't think that he's seen us yet, but there's no way we can walk out in front of him without some kind of diversion. I see it's time for the mercenaries' demonstration. Could you ask them if they could possibly aim it down this way today, please? Thank you, dear."

Hanging up, she turned and grinned in a feral fashion at Morgan. "That gate guard will have a lot more on his hands than he's expecting. Now, we wait. Be ready for my cue-keep your hood up, stay close to me and be ready to move fast when I tell you to."

In the distance, Morgan heard a thunderous roar that sounded like a riot or a catastrophe or a scrum of football hooligans on parade surging towards the bathroom where they were hiding. Peering out, she saw a sea of armored figures waving swords and maces in vigorous and enthusiastic combat careening down the path in their direction. Visitors and town folk alike leapt like gazelles out of the path of the battle, and then fell in behind the carnage to see what was going on.

As the battle crashed past the lady's room, the woman slipped out of the door and moved with it, gesturing for Morgan to follow. Feeling exposed and vulnerable, Morgan pulled her hood closer about her face and ran after her.

At the gate, the watching sidhe was leaning forward, looking intently for his target amongst the approaching chaos. Suddenly he leapt back, face contorted with fear, as an iron sword swept past his nose. Morgan realized that most of the weapons flailing freely about in the scrimmage around her were made of steel-and that steel was made up in part of cold iron.

"The benefits of a liberal education and of reading filler in the paper." thought Morgan. "You learn things like this."

For a number of moments, the unseelie hunter shrieked loudly and danced vigorously about, avoiding contact with the perilous metal. He was too busy with saving his skin to be bothered with who was entering or leaving the faire; and the crowds that gathered to watch the melee gave more cover to the women quietly making their way to the gate.

As they slipped through the gate, Morgan heard a loud huzzah and the sound of a hundred swords being beaten on as many shields in celebration of the conflict's resolution. She also heard a final unseelie shriek ring out, and grinned broadly within her hood.

"Very satisfying." she said.

Her companion smiled broadly. "Isn't it? Well, here we are." she said. "Now where is that van?"

As they cleared the gate house, a blue van with a dragon's head bobber pulled up rapidly to the gate. The door flew open, and a familiar face peered out, grinning.

"Your carriage awaits, my lady," the mustached man said, gesturing grandly.

"Never mind that" cried the woman, bundling Morgan into the passenger's side and slamming the door. "Head down, keep moving, and make sure you watch out for other vehicles following! Make sure you don't pick up followers-you're taking her to a friend's house."

"Stay safe, my dear." she said, stepping back as the van pulled quickly away.

Looking in the mirror, Morgan saw the woman stand staring after the van for a moment, then draw herself up and turn towards the gate. The golden glow began to expand around her, deeper, brighter and more powerful than before. The woman stalked towards the gate, with shoulders set and her body braced, and re-entered.

Morgan saw a flare of golden light burst from the gate; and then they pulled around the corner and were out of sight.

"Will they be all right?" she asked her driver. "Those hunters are dangerous. She and her husband came between the hunters and me. Will they be safe?"

"They've been fine up to now" he smiled, taking a corner on two wheels, then immediately taking another to see if he was being followed. "Not to make light of your situation, but you're certainly not the first person they've helped, and that's not the first menace they've faced. From my experience, they'd probably be able to manage if it were just the two of them-and at the faire, they've got a whole bunch of friends that would come bursting out of the woodwork if they were seriously in trouble.

"I think that anyone who tries to cause trouble for them will be the ones who end up with trouble." he said. "Be at ease now, my lady. They'll be fine. The question is more how you're doing."

She had to think about that. "I've been better." She admitted. "But things are improving quickly"

"And, in the spirit of things improving quickly," he said "I'm pleased to be able to inform you that we seem to have gotten away without anyone in pursuit. Now then, where might we be going?"

She reached into her pocket and pulled out the map. "Here's the address" she said, showing him. "Do you need directions?"

"Nay, milady. I'll just tap my little gremlin here on the head" he said, patting a GPS, "and he'll magically show me the way. Take your ease. You're safe with me, and we'll have you there soon."

Morgan pulled the cloak closer around her, and relaxed into the seat. It felt like she'd been running forever, even though it was only a few days. It was a pleasure to rest and regain her center a bit, although she knew this little chunk of moving sanctuary wouldn't last for long. She closed her eyes for just a moment...

Thirty-Five
Morgan

She woke to the sound of the van pulling up in front of a little house secluded in the trees on a quiet little lane. The air was clean and crisp, and seemed to tingle. Lights shone in the windows, and the front door opened as her driver turned off the engine.

"I'll just walk you to the door, and then I have to be heading back," he said. "Now are you sure you're going be all right?"

"No, I'm not," said Morgan honestly. "But this is something I need to see through. Will you take this cloak back for me? I didn't get a chance to return it, with all the hurry."

"It's my pleasure to serve you in any way I can," he said grandly. He opened the door for her, helping her from the van. Taking her arm grandly, he walked her up to the front porch where a tall redheaded woman stood waiting.

"Fair ye well, milady, and may the rest of your journey be a boring one." He bent low to kiss her hand and then strode magnificently away into darkness.

The two women looked after him. "He's rather dramatic" said the redhead "but he has a good heart. Anyway, come in and shut the night out. Be thou welcome to my home. The tarot reader called ahead about you and any friend of my friends is my friend as well. Speaking of friends, I've got someone here who I hear you know…"

Inside the door, the house was old and worn but well-loved, with a feeling of sanctuary and nurturing. Worn but comfortable furniture, full to overflowing bookshelves, treasured knickknacks displayed with pride-all Morgan saw combined as a place of quirky individuality, less concerned with impressing and more with welcoming. The energy was cool and clear and calm-and Morgan could see a faint white glow in the air around her.

Morgan loved it at once. She felt safe here.

Cats mewed from the staircase and peered at her from behind chairs. An excitable little dog ran up to her and jumped up, begging to be petted. Another dog, larger, slower, ambled up, nudging past the first with a massive head, insisting on her share of the attention. Morgan smiled and knelt to pet them both in turn.

"I see the ladies have introduced themselves, and the gentlemen are peering around the corner at you." said her hostess. "I think, though, that we've got someone else waiting for you. Come this way" she said, gesturing towards a shadowed, curtained archway.

Morgan rose and followed her. Beyond the curtains, she found herself in a cozy, dimly lit little room. Beds ran along two of the walls, quiet new age music played, and floor pillows were scattered about, making a welcoming sanctuary for man or beast. Morgan noticed crystals in the room's four corners, as well as carefully placed in other locations. Even the air in the room felt clearer, cleaner, so full of positive energy you could almost touch it. Morgan breathed in, and felt stronger, more centered and at peace.

She heard a strangled sound-half mew, half gasp. She turned in the direction of the sound, and, looking down, saw Sam, curled up on one of the throw pillows. He was battered and burned, but oddly enough, the wounds all had the look of having happened weeks ago.

"Sam!" she cried, throwing herself to the floor beside him. "Are you o.k.? I thought I'd never see you again!" He winced as she tried to pet him, then raised his head and nuzzled her. She carefully placed her hand on his head, and, when he did not wince again, gently began to scritch behind the ears in his favorite spot.

Sam purred. The red headed woman withdrew discreetly through the archway.

"So, what happened?" they both exclaimed simultaneously, and then both burst into laughter. He nodded for her to go first.

"When you told me to run and leave you behind, I did, but I didn't want to. I did because all you'd done to save me would have been wasted if I didn't, but I felt like I was betraying you by running away." said Morgan.

"No, my girl, you did fine." said Sam. "You were who they wanted, and if they finished you, that could mean the end of everything. As a cat, I'm naturally important, but for once, you were more important than I was."

"Once you ran, they followed you. I couldn't help you anymore then, because I was too hurt to catch up, but I wasn't too injured to crawl away and hide once they weren't looking; and that's what saved my life. That, and a pretty little Goth girl, who found me and brought me here to the excellent healer in the other room."

"But, what happened to you?" he asked. "When I was wounded, the best advice I could give you was to run for your life, but I was still scared they were going to catch you. You're new to this, you don't have all the knowledge you need, you're not used to dodging unseelie assassins, and without me to guide you, I feared that I'd seen the last of you. How did you give them the slip?" he asked.

"It wasn't easy." she admitted. "I ran like mad, and dodged in and out of a number of places, including the big department store downtown. When I lost them for a bit and got time to think, I remembered the tarot reader I saw earlier this week. He'd offered help if I needed, and, when I looked at his website, I saw that he was working a renaissance faire today. I hopped a bus to the faire, and found him. He gave me some information, including telling me that you were alive and where to find you. He also, together with his wife, and a lot of their friends, managed to distract the hunters looking for me, and get me safely away from the faire, transporting me from there to here."

"And here I am," she said. So what do we do now? How are you? You look very weak. Are you safe here? Are you in danger? Will those hunters come bursting through the door to attack you? For that matter, will those hunters come bursting through the door to attack me? Am I putting you and everyone here in danger by being here? Maybe I need to go, so I won't draw danger to any of you."

"No." said a voice at the door. Morgan turned and the healer was there. "You and your friend are safe here. The land, house itself, and this room again are all individually warded, which should provide considerable protection against the sidhe."

"Warding? What's that?" asked Morgan.

"It's a way of protecting the boundaries of an area such as a room, house or area of land to keep out beings, energies and things you don't want coming in. In our case, that would be harmful, evil or unseelie ones. Wards can also keep things in. In addition, our wards also conceal what's inside of them, so those who are hunting you can't detect you."

"Besides that, this farmhouse is well over two hundred years old, and has been lived in by loving families for most of the time. For this reason, its natural boundaries are very strong, because it is most definitely a home, and not simply a building or a way station. It possesses a powerful hearth spirit, which carefully watches over the safety and well-being of those who live here, as well as those invited in."

"And, we've other defenses as well," she said, and, for a moment, she looked larger, stronger, more formidable. Then Morgan blinked, and her hostess was back to how she'd appeared before.

"Those are some reasons your friend was safe here. I take in the wounded and those in need of healing, and sometimes that means I need to be able to protect them, so they can heal. That's why you'd both be safe here for as long as you chose to stay. My impression, though, is" the red headed woman continued "that you have further places to go and not much time to get there. Is that so?"

Morgan stared at her like a deer in the headlights. How much did this woman know? How much could she be trusted?

The red headed woman looked at her for a moment, and then laughed in a friendly fashion. "Oh, the look on your face!" she said. "My lady, you have nothing to fear from me. I'm a healer in service to the Light, and I wish you nothing but well. That's why your friends, the readers, sent you here. That's why your friend was brought to me. If

I served the Darkness, Sam would no longer be alive, for he certainly wasn't in any shape to save himself from harm when he was brought here."

"And you can talk with him in front of me if you like. I know that he is not an **ordinary** cat."

Morgan turned to Sam, who grinned weakly at her. "It's true. My cover's blown." He admitted. "I was in and out of consciousness when I first got here, and evidently I talk in my sleep. Having watched her, though, I shouldn't have been surprised if she picked it upon her own."

"He gave me quite a start," said the woman. "but it was nice to have someone to talk to while my husband's away. Going back to the original issue though, you're certainly welcome to stay here. You'd definitely be safe. But, I'm somehow thinking that you're not going to."

Morgan hung her head.

"I'd like to" she said. "I've been dumped into this very fast, I seriously don't know what I'm doing, and I'm really scared that I'm going to get myself or someone else killed. From what Sam tells me, though, I have to keep going. I evidently carry a tiny bit of the power of the elven court within me, and my presence or absence at the court could tip the scales so darkness rules this world."

"I'd like to stay. I don't want to go. But I have to."

The red headed woman shook her head. "I see. That's quite a problem you have there. I've a lot of respect for a woman who'll do the right thing, rather than what's safest or easiest. So what can I do to help you then?"

"Well, I don't know about you." snarled Sam "but I'm going to see her safely to court!" He tried to stand up, and cried out involuntarily with pain.

"Not good…" the healer said, giving him a look.

"You can't do that," said Morgan. "You're too badly hurt. It'd kill you to be out running around out there, and I can't bear to lose you again."

"It's my job," said Sam "and a cat's gotta do what a cat's gotta do." With effort, he stood up again, stretching and wincing with effort. His movements, tentative at first, became smoother and more powerful as he worked his muscles, and the signs of pain grew less.

"It'll do," he said in a few minutes. "I'll hate myself in the morning, but it'll do what I need to do."

The healer knelt. "I'm with her," she said, nodding towards Morgan. "This is a bad idea, but I've yet to see a cat who can be dissuaded from doing what it chooses. Let me see if I can help a little bit."

She closed her eyes and held her hands out over Sam's head for a moment. The air in the room got warmer, and Morgan's left eye saw waves of color flowing from her palms to the cat. Sam's body relaxed and he began to purr.

"Now try" said the healer, opening her eyes again. Sam stretched again, and his stiffness was almost gone. "That'll do" he said. "Now I'm fit for the road."

"Well, be careful on that road." said the healer, getting up."Your body can only take so much punishment."

She reached into her pocket and pulled something out. "Here are the keys to my car. You're going to need to cover ground and cover it fast, and my beast should help you do that and give you some protection while you do so. Take good care of it, and yourselves as well, and bring it back when you're done with it."

"I'm overwhelmed." said Morgan. "Thank you so

much for everything you've done for Sam and me. You've saved his life, and I can't ever thank you enough for that. I don't know what I would do without him."

The healer snorted. "Thank me if we all survive this. The thought of it-a cat on a tear, careening around the country side against doctor's advice."

"Clock's ticking and adventure's waiting. We'd best be getting out there if we want to get there in time," said the cat, "Come on, Morgan. Let's boogie!" He shot from the room, velocity lines stretching out behind him.

Morgan got up more slowly, taking the car keys from the healer and tucking them in her pocket.

"Thank you again for everything you've done for us." She said. "I really do appreciate it."

The healer smiled "Thank you for all you're doing for all of us as well." she said. "To do my work, I need a beautiful and kindly world to work in. What you're doing ensures that."

"Only if I succeed." thought Morgan.

She looked longingly around for one last time at the cozy room, the welcoming house, the final safe space she knew of on her journey. Straightening her shoulders, she walked to the door and opened it, walking away from safety and into the night.

Outside, the golden cat dashed ahead of her to the car, and jumped up and in as soon as she opened the door.

"Shotgun! I claim shotgun!" shouted Sam.

"You fuzzy idiot," Morgan said fondly. "You can't drive. Your paws won't even touch the pedals."

The healer watched them drive away. "God bless them" she thought, "and all of us besides.

Thirty-Six
Morgan

Once they'd pulled away from the healer's home and were on their way back to town, they realized they were out in the back of nowhere in the farm lands and the forests that bordered the city. Both of them had been asleep when they arrived at the healer's house, and, neither one of them had paid close attention to the verbal directions the healer had given them on how return to town before they'd left the house and walked out to the car .

Morgan thought their inattention was due to stress and exhaustion. Sam refused to take any responsibility for directions at all, and just sat there on the front seat looking mysterious.

It was good to be back together again.

They'd been driving for a half an hour now, threading their way through darkened streets and unfamiliar boulevards and down cul de sacs, looking at street markers, and trying to find their way back to the center of town where the gate was next scheduled to open the following morning. At least twice now they'd had to stop under street lights, unfolding the map that they'd found in the glove compartment and arguing companionably over where they were at the moment and the best route to get to where they were going. The streets were empty of traffic and any other activity at this cold and lonely time of night. It was the middle of the night, and the silence of folks asleep spilled out into the moonlight.

Since the streets were empty and the trip was relatively quiet (except for the number of wrong turns they took), they had plenty of time to talk.

"I missed you, Sam." said Morgan.

There was a long pause.

"And I missed you too, Morgan." said Sam.

"No, Sam-I *really* missed you." said Morgan more intensely. "Not like "I went out for sushi and now that I'm back, I'm glad to see you". I *really missed you.*"

"When we were separated in the city, I thought that you were gone and I was never going to see you again. I thought you were dead. I thought you were dead because you tried to save my life."

"I've never felt so alone in all my life."

A tear ran slowly down one of Morgan's cheeks. The golden cat gently put one paw on her knee as she drove, and looked intently up at her face.

"I've always known that I cared about you," Morgan said "but I didn't realize how much until I thought that you were gone for good. *I really, really missed you.* And, since I've had a miracle now and gotten a second chance, I wanted to be sure to tell you how important you're to me."

Sam rubbed his head up against her elbow affectionately.

"I know that, girl." he said roughly. "I was worried about you as well. I missed you, my Morgan, and I'm glad that we're back together as a team."

"Besides" he said more brightly "there's absolutely no way you'd get through this whole adventure without me, so there's no way I could leave you now or at any time in the future. You've still got plenty of things to learn about magick and adventure, my girl, so there's no way whatsoever that you're getting rid of this cat now or any time. Got it, girl friend?"

Morgan giggled despite herself, serious mood broken.

"Got it!" she said, and drove on, smile on her face.

"Good then!" said Sam, and cuddled up against her side, purring like a sports car.

There was a prolonged companionable lack of conversation while she drove.

"So exactly what did happen to you while I was out of circulation?" asked Sam eventually.

There was a lot of answer to that particular question. Morgan took a minute to organize her thoughts about what she'd say, and then opened her mouth, preparing to begin…

And then they heard a noise approaching from off in the distance.

The noise was startling after all the silence they'd been driving through. It was a buzzing noise, an irritating whining like oversized mosquitoes in a hurry.

"Motorcycles." said Sam, after due consideration. "Motorcycles headed in our direction. And, while it may be that a couple of the boys are just heading home after a very late night out, on the whole, I think it might be as well for us to be cautious about this. Morgan, do you see any place that we might lay low for the moment?"

Morgan had already been looking urgently around her as she drove, looking for a good place for them to take cover. While not totally paranoid, she thought Sam's caution was well founded, given the recent events in their lives. There weren't really many places to hide a vehicle though out in the burbs, especially hiding places with multiple options; and, given her last two days, Morgan wanted every single option that she could lay her hands on at this and any moment.

She was beginning to feel a bit panicked.

They could see the glow of multiple headlights beaming up into the darkened sky overhead several streets over. Several streets over, but winding in their direction and coming altogether too fast for her liking…

Morgan switched off her car headlights, to make them harder to spot or track, and drove by the light of the streetlights alone.

Both of them were looking for a hiding place now, heads swiveling fiercely from side to side, eyes darting back and forth, looking for some place, any place they could conceal a small hybrid car without trapping themselves with no place to go, if hiding didn't work out.

The sound and the lights of the motor bikes were getting closer by the moment…

"There!" said Morgan sharply, holding hysteria out of her voice by sheer effort. "Over there, down the side street! "

There to the side, down a cul de sac with a circle at the end of it, someone had evidently started a major home repair project, and had a dumpster parked in the street to take care of the mound of refuse. It was a dead end, but there was room to maneuver if discovered, and the darkness behind the dumpster would make them harder to spot

Morgan made a sharp turn and whipped down to turn in the circle and to park herself in the shelter of the dumpster, well hidden from the main street. She killed the engine and she and Sam sat waiting together in the shadow of the dumpster in nervous silence.

The sounds of roaring motor bikes drew closer and closer and finally came cruising around the far corner on the street they'd just been driving down a few moments before. Raucous laughter and shouted comments drifted down the street, rising above the sound of the high powered engines.

The car they were in was hidden from the main street by the rusty bulk of the dumpster, but, from where she was seated if she sat at just the right angle, Morgan could catch a glimpse of the end of the street around the side of the huge metal container. She leaned over slightly to get a better look, to watch for anything that made it wise to start the car again and drive like mad, and then froze in that awkward position, so there'd be no movement to visually call attention to where they were hidden.

Sam and Morgan sat in the darkness, breath held tight, waiting for the bikes to pass on by so that they could move on again.

The noise and light grew closer and closer, until, at last, the bikes passed by the end of the cul de sac. Metal and chrome glistened against the dark in the beams of the cycle headlights. The roar of powerful engines filled the air, so much that Morgan was amazed that no one called the police or leaned out of an upstairs window to complain.

From her vantage point hidden behind the dumpster, Morgan watched the motor cycle gang drive by; and there were enough of them that she was glad that they had found a place to take cover before the gang had seen them.

And then, for some undetermined reason, she closed

the right eye, and looked at the passing cavalcade with only her "seeing" eye.

And, all at once, everything changed for her...

With both eyes open, what she saw was a passing motor cycle gang on massive Harleys, tough and rugged, burly intimidating men dressed in studded dark leathers with helmets and goggles that hid their eyes; but, when she closed one eye and looked only through the one that held enchanted sight, she saw a different story.

Elves, tall and pale, with faces fair but deadly, dressed in silks and satins and armor of most curious design. Helmets on their heads as well, but helmets of ethereal yet savage shapes, made for prestige and for combat. Elves, mounted not on heavy motor cycles, but on fabulous steeds, clad in curious barding and with extravagant comparison depending from their harnesses and saddles. Elves that jingled and shone as they rode, as fair as Death, on unearthly horses with eldritch hounds running along at their sides.

Elves that laughed and shouted and catcalled one to another as they rode along hunting. And their voices had no sign of a friendly sound to it.

And as they rode, one hound turned its head towards them, its nose fast at work in the darkness, turned towards them and sniffed and whined. She froze, as if being stiller than still would help her to be even less apparent to the hunting dog.

The dog stopped in its tracks. It turned its head towards the dead end street where they were hiding, and it whined eagerly again

Morgan's breath caught in her chest.

And then, with a loud exclamation and a rough oath, an elven huntsmen wrenched at the lead of the hound, and pulled him back into line with the rest of the hunting train. The hound continued to stare back down their street with shining red eyes as it was pulled along.

A hunting horn blew loudly-and Morgan closed her remaining eye tight and sank back silently into the depths of the seat of the car, blanking her mind into the prey's natural mind set of "…don't find me don't find me…"

A soft paw touched her arm, and her eyes flew open, as she almost shrieked with alarm.

Sam stretched up quickly and placed his other paw on her lips; and the two of them huddled together there quietly in the sheltering darkness for minutes that felt like eternity, before the last riders of the hunt finally passed by their hiding place…

They listened to the hunt ride on, going farther and farther away from them in the distance, until at last, they were gone.

And then, cat and mistress collapsed together laughing hysterically in the front seat of the car in the darkness, muscles releasing from tension that the hadn't realized they were holding, breath exploding from too held lungs .

"Well, that was altogether too close for any degree of comfort." wheezed Sam finally.

Morgan found a crumpled tissue and wiped away some of the tears that were streaming from her own eyes.

"Just another part of the rich panoply that's currently my life." she said to him. "Perhaps we'd better be moving on again, before those bozos come back, and we're in major trouble."

Still laughing a bit, she cautiously started the engine, turned on the lights and pulled out around the dumpster, heading the car off in the opposite direction from that which the elven train had taken.

Thirty-Seven
Morgan

It was less than a half hour later, and the midnight winds were blowing wisps of clouds across the gibbous moon, when they heard the sound of motorcycles roaring in their direction again.

Sam and Morgan looked frantically at each other, and then started looking wildly around, trying to figure out which direction the incoming riders were coming from. Morgan tuned off the car headlights again to make them less visible, and drove by the light of the street lights, as they looked for a good place to hide.

By now, they'd made their way through much of the farm lands and suburbs on the edges of the community, and were coming into a downtown commercial district, largely abandoned at night save for occasional police patrols. Tall buildings towered around them. The sound of engines echoed down the concrete canyons, making it hard to figure out which direction the hunt was coming from, or how close they were.

"I just can't tell where they're coming from." said Morgan desperately.

Sam said "Me neither. But we need a place to hide, and quick!"

There were plenty decent hiding places, dependant on the situation. The problem was that, since they couldn't tell where the hunt was coming from, it was hard to pick a spot that would give them the best cover.

"Hurry up, Morgan! Pick a spot!" shouted Sam. "They're almost here."

"We still can't tell where they're coming from…" replied Morgan. "…so how can I pick the right spot? "

And at that point, they ran out of time…

On the cross street one block ahead, they saw motor headlights radiating down the street. The echoes finally came together in one blast of sound coming from the same direction.

Motorcycles, barely a block away. They were definitely out of time.

Sam looked wildly about them. No cross streets before the one the motor bikes were on. No open driveways to drive into. No dumpsters on the street to hide behind. There was no decent place to conceal themselves.

They were properly and officially screwed…

All at once, she had an idea. She pulled the car over to the curb, parked it in the shadows between two other cars, and turned off the engine, leaving the keys in the ignition.

"Just what on earth are you doing?!" screamed Sam. "They're almost here!"

Morgan turned to him calmly. "I know that," she said. "Now be quiet and get down!" She put her hand on top of his head and firmly pushed him down below the window before lying down on the passenger's seat herself. Reaching up quickly, she quickly twisted the rear view mirror forwards before dropping her hand below the dashboard again.

Sam's jaw dropped as he realized what she was doing.

"Brilliant." he whispered under his breath.

"Thank you." she said quietly. "Now, hush!" And

she pressed her lips tightly together as they waited for the elves.

From her reclining position, Morgan was hidden behind the dashboard and car doors from any casual viewer passing on the street. If they stayed still, the shadow in which she'd parked would give them even more concealment; but, from where she lay, she could still see the street behind their car in the side view mirrors. Given the angle she'd twisted the rear view mirror above her, she had a small but choice view of the street ahead of her as well. She could see the cross street with the light of approaching motorcycles on it. She'd be able to see the sidhe as they passed, and she'd be able to see if they turned to come down the street that she and Sam were parked on.

She might see if the unseelie spotted them – possibly even in enough time to do something useful and meaningful that might help the two of them survive.

Beneath her hand, Sam was lying stock still, save only for his ears, which were alternatively swiveling back and forth, and fixating trying to gain as much information as possible.

"They're almost to this street now." he whispered to her under his breath. "It sounds like there's not as many of them this time as before. They must have split up their bigger rade into several smaller hunting parties."

"That's good for us." said Morgan quietly "as long as we don't run away from one group and bump into another one. Now let's stay quiet and hope they don't spot us."

Both of them lay on the front seat of the car, their senses alert and their breath held tight within them. The oncoming lights grew brighter, and the engine noise louder, as the motorcycles approached the intersection, and the tension built appreciably in the car.

Morgan had looked the unseelie hunt with her "seeing" eye the last time the hunters had ridden by. She knew that, while they looked like motorcycles, the mounts of the unseelie were really esoteric horses in elaborate barding and comparison.

Too much fear can make your mind do funny things. As Morgan lay there on the seat, in mortal terror, she found herself wondering about the noises of the engines, since the mounts were not really motor cycles. What was making that roaring sound? Was it just that this was what an onlooker expected to hear, and therefore what they did hear? Was the sound an illusion, an elven glamour of some sort? Were the horses actually going "vroom, vroom" for their own entertainment or for that of their riders?

Almost hysterically, Morgan mentally resolved to ask Sam to explain about all of this to her, if they both survived the night.

The beams were growing even brighter now, and converging together as they do when the source of a light is almost upon you. The intersection was bright and shining with imminence.

The shining chrome wheel and the fork of the first motorcycle rolled into her sight in the intersection ahead of them, followed closely by six of his brothers of the road.

Seven unseelie elves mounted on motorcycles, impossibly fair and unquestionably deadly, slowly rolled into the intersection in front of their car, slowly circling counter clockwise in an almost dreamlike movement, as if trying to find a trail. The dog running effortlessly at their side cast about on the ground, whining in his eagerness, searching for signs of their quarry.

Morgan shuddered inwardly. She was very glad that they had not already passed that way, and that there were no traces of their passage there to find.

Circling…circling…circling…

And then, abruptly, coming to a stop.

Seven unseelie elves in a loose circle beneath the blinking caution light. The light threw flickering shadows across their sharp faces like transitory war paint, emphasizing their fierceness and inhuman beauty. They turned their bikes and faced outwards, one to each of the four quarters and three in the center, and the smoky hound slunk back and forth around the circle between his unseelie masters, ears down and tail held firmly between his legs, whining and sniffing the air.

They stayed there for just a moment, testing the air, and Morgan froze in position, willing with all her strength that their attention would pass over Sam and herself and miss them.

With a startling roar of engines that almost shocked her into crying out, the riders pulled slowly away from the intersection, fanning out, two of them cruising slowly down each cross street not already travelled, and one remaining in the cross roads, keeping a careful watch. Each unseelie sidhe looked alertly about him as he cruised, looking for signs and tracks that would betray a prey worth hunting.

The car that Morgan and Sam were hiding in was half way down the block, between an SUV and a station wagon. She couldn't see where the hound had run to because of her limited field of vision, but she could clearly see the hunting elves approaching slowly in the twisted rear view mirror.

That was terrifying enough for the moment. She could only hope that the shadows of SUV and buildings and as much stillness as they could manage would be enough to keep them safe from unseelie eyes.

The elven riders rode gradually down the street, one on each side of the road, cold eyes flicking from side to side. The unseelie sidhe on their side came closer and closer until his face dropped out of the space reflected in the rearview mirror.

And then, she could see his face through the outside corner of the windshield.

She felt like her pale white face was shining in the half light, like it was a luminous beacon that must inevitably give her away to the hunter. She wanted nothing so much as to turn her face and bury it into the seat to hide it from the sidhe; but some small part of her brain still sane knew that if she moved a millimeter, the movement would be more obvious than the contrast of her skin in the darkness. Instead she froze, staring up at the elf gliding by less than two feet from her.

The engine growled and snarled as the bike moved slowly down the street. The face of the elven hunter slid from the corner of her windshield on into the side window. His eyes, alert and scanning for signs of prey, came back towards this side of the street.

And then they glanced over the top of her and moved on. As did the elf himself.

"What happened?" screamed Morgan's mind. "He looked right at me! How the heck did he miss me?"

Then she realized that she was now underneath the elven hunters' normal field of vision, and because they'd frozen like rabbits and neither moved or made any sound, there was nothing to draw his attention down lower.

From where she lay motionless, she now saw the back of the elf slowly receding on his motorcycle in the wing mirrors, only slightly obscured by the "Objects in mirror are closer than they appear" legend.

She thought that she'd never seen anything quite so beautiful in all of her life...

She relaxed slightly for a moment, although still remaining still and motionless. No need to draw unwanted attention to herself. She relaxed for two, while she was at it. She'd really earned those moments.

And she watched in her rearview mirror, as the back view of the elven hunter pulled away from her on his motor cycle, smaller and farther away by the moment.

Then she heard the sound just outside the driver's side door of the car. There was a soft snuffling first, the sound of something sniffing at the outside of the car. A whine. A soft bump, like something running up against the door panel. Another bump, followed by a slight scratching of nails on the car body.

"Damn! The dog!" cursed Morgan mentally. She'd forgotten about the dog.

In the side view mirror, she saw the eleven warrior

slow down and come to a stop. He began to slowly turn around.

There was another soft bump on the car door; another muffled whine; a further noise of the scrabbling of claws...

And the head of the hound arose over the edge of the frame, baring his teeth at her and looking directly through the side window at both of them.

He stared at them for a moment with burning red eyes; and then he threw back his head and howled. And all the Unseelie sidhe threw back their heads and howled back at the top of their lungs in response...

Morgan sat bolt upright in her seat and lunged for the key in the ignition...

Thirty-Eight
Elsewhere

A tiny pixie, snatched away from her sheltered nest.

A slender kelpie, dragged from the river's depths and beaten viciously into insensibility.

A trooping faerie, vanished completely from all of her usual haunts.

And, one by one, more and more quickly, those who were carrying the power for the Light were going missing.

They were simply gone…

The Lands That Lie Between

Thirty-Nine
Morgan

...And all of the unseelie sidhe threw back their heads and howled back at the top of their lungs in response to the hound.

Morgan sat bolt upright in her seat and lunged for the key in the ignition.

The unseelie dog howled again; and foamed and snarled and loudly crashed its forelegs against the window, trying to break it to get to them. The glass cracked slightly, a spider web of delicate cracks radiating from the initial impact.

The car engine roared loudly, returning to life under her panicked cranking of the car key. Morgan frantically wrenched at the steering wheel, swinging the car to the left, out of the parking space and towards the savage dog. There was a loud thump and a yelp, and the hound vanished out of the window.

Morgan winced. She hated to hurt anything, even an Unseelie dog trying to attack them. She'd have preferred to just stay hidden until the danger had passed them by; but it was far too late for that. Far too late to be subtle. Far too late to stay hidden from the unseelie hunters.

Her jaw set. She hated to hurt anything, but it was clear that those hunting them had no such qualms. She might have to hurt them to protect Sam and keep from being hurt herself.

The elven hunter whipped his head around, fully alerted now, and, his cycle roared in challenge to the car she was driving. His fellow hunter who was patrolling across the street from him also turned rapidly, and Morgan could hear the sounds of the other five riders also returning to join in the hunt.

She didn't wait to see or hear anything more. Still cockeyed in her seat, she rammed her foot to the floor. The car leapt forwards, accelerating like a rocket on the fourth of July, and leaving her stomach far behind in a little quivering heap.

Behind her, Morgan heard another savage howl go up. Quickly reaching up, she twisted the rearview mirror hard, so she could better see what was chasing her. The mirror popped into place, and the face of the first sidhe was in it, larger than life. Morgan startled. It almost looked like he was sitting in the back seat. His eyes were large and shining with savage joy, and he was smiling, a smile less about pleasantry and more about baring one's teeth.

This was someone who loved his work. Morgan resolved to make his working conditions as thoroughly unpleasant for him as humanly possible.

She continued to pick up speed as the car found its mojo deep within the heart of its engine. Behind her, the hunters fell into formation, shouting and laughing, as they raced after her. In the mirror, Morgan noticed abstractedly that the illusion was slipping. Sometimes she could see motorcycles and sometimes great grey ghostly horses with burning red eyes.

There was no sign of the hound at least.

Morgan found she felt vaguely guilty about that. She liked dogs. She would never hurt a dog. Unless, of course, it was trying to climb in her car window and bite her throat out. At that point, all bets were off.

"Still" she thought, her mind going into shock and babbling, as minds will do at such times, "no doubt he was a reasonably nice unseelie hound, efficient at his job perhaps, beloved by friends and associates, a pillar of the community, somebody's pup at one point or the other. I hope that the poor dog is all right."

Meanwhile, the little car continued to accelerate under the unconscious guidance of her frantic hands to a pace beyond its normal speed. Whooping loudly, the two elves also speeded up behind her, cycles roaring, horses bugling; and their fellows had wheeled and were approaching the car rapidly from the left and from directly in front of her.

Morgan noticed with the small corner of her brain that wasn't otherwise occupied that the elves behind her were gaining and would flank her soon if she didn't do something about it.

"They're going to come upon either side of me," the analytical part of her brain not shrieking with fear observed. "and if they do, I'm not sure what they have planned , but I'm reasonably sure it won't be a good thing for us. I think I'd better not let them do that…"

Morgan wrenched hard at the wheel of the car once more and began to swerve vigorously back and forth across the road–not covering the darkened road completely but more than enough to make passing on either side a challenging and hazardous feat. Startled, the flanking elves also began to swing wide to avoid a crushing impact with her fenders.

Beside her on the passenger seat and not buckled in, Sam was thrown violently from side to side.

"Ooof!" he yowled in pain. "Ow! Morgan, could you...ack!...slow down...ow!...just a minute, dear...argh!...and let me get myself...ack...situated here just a bit?!"

Morgan felt sorry for him. She felt his pain...but she also felt sure that, if she slowed the car, they'd both be feeling a different kind of pain that neither one of them would care for. As a compromise, she reached out with the classic old school "mom–stabilizing–package–about–to–tip–over–while–driving" grip, beloved throughout the centuries by people who "just couldn't stop now". Eyes on the road, she blindly reached to the side with one hand, driving furiously with the other, until she could feel the sensation of flying fur. She bore down firmly enough to stabilize Sam until he could get a grip on something himself and stop flying around the car. Meanwhile, with her other hand, she kept swerving furiously, doing her best to keep the elves from passing, all while the small analytical portion of her brain still working tried to come up with a plan; something; anything to deal with the other oncoming assailants.

Even driving through Boston had not totally prepared her for this (although it had built some solid skills she was using at the moment.)

The two flanking sidhe had developed a working rhythm. As she would veer towards one of them, he would swing outwards and his fellow on the other side would veer inwards and gain a little ground on her. In the meanwhile, the three hunters coming from straight ahead were getting closer, and the other two sidhe was swinging wide around the corner of the street up ahead, and powering after them.

"Just not going to happen." thought Morgan, and changed her tactics again.

She'd fallen into a rhythm, back and forth, to keep the elves pacing her from passing; but time was running. She started to verge left as she had been, and then suddenly and unexpectedly wrenched the wheel to the right. Hard.

There was the sound of a heavy impact and an agonized shriek, as the elf on that side met her bumper up close and personal. The shocked face of the hunter dropped out of sight in the rear passenger window, and, snatching a glance in the rear view mirror, Morgan caught the impression of a motor cycle sliding headlong on its side in one direction while a body tumbled limply in another.

"That's one down." thought Morgan, and immediately turned the wheel in the other direction, catching her other flanker in the instant he was looking back at the downed biker himself. There was another cry of pain and surprise, another heavy impact, and another motor cycle skidding noisily on its side along the pavement behind her in a minute.

"Two." she thought, and the ghost of a smile tickled at one corner of her mouth. "We just might possibly make it out of this one alive."

"They don't like that, you know." said Sam casually as he wedged himself under the seat belt.

"No surprise that." said Morgan, as she drove towards the oncoming elves. "I wouldn't like being hit by a car myself, never mind sliding on my side down a road at highway speeds on a motorcycle suddenly intent on crushing me."

Sam looked abashed.

"Well, there's that, of course," he remarked. "But, there's also the fact that most of the body of this car is made out of steel. And a major component of steel is…"

"…cold iron." said Morgan, suddenly getting what he was saying. "Someone I met while we were separated said something about some elves having problems with cold iron."

"These boys are evidently just that kind of elf." shouted Sam, as he clung desperately to the seat upholstery of the rocking car. "Think about it for a minute, Morgan. Not only have you hit them with a ton and a half blunt object, you've hit them with a ton and a half blunt object made of cold iron. All in all, it's not that surprising that they're kind of cranky about the whole thing."

Morgan's eyes opened wide, as the little car rocketed towards the oncoming unseelie. The concept of cold iron in play was one that opened up a whole new range of opportunities in their situation to her.

The first of the oncoming sidhe had dropped an eight foot lance into position for skewering the driver through the windshield as he rode by the speeding vehicle. As the tip of the lance passed over the car's hood, Morgan wrenched the steering wheel hard to the left, moving the lance tip out of line with her face and catching it with the base of the car aerial, so the lance snapped. Splinters of broken lance flew out in all directions, including up against the windshield, cracking it slightly in several places. The elven hunter, knocked off balance, lurched violently to the side and disappeared, mount and rider, sliding under the front of the speeding car at high speed in a cloud of sparks.

There was a screech and a violent bump from

beneath the car as they passed.

"That'll be three…" thought Morgan, and kept driving.

His scouting partner was coming head on at her, lagging only slightly behind his fellow sidhe. She swerved back again to try and drive him off of the road as well, but he managed to evade her, passing and then turning quickly around to follow behind her.

The head lights of the other three oncoming motorcycles shone in her eyes, and she could see the lone sidhe crowding behind her back bumper. They were running out of options fast.

"Where are the police?" shouted Sam from the passenger's seat. "Shouldn't they be here enforcing traffic safety or something? Don't they know that you pay taxes?"

The oncoming bikers were almost upon them.

"I think that the police only patrol here at certain specific times," said Morgan, her mind racing and scrabbling wildly for survival options. "and I guess this is not one of the times. Besides, since I've been running bikers off the road, I don't know if police attention would be a totally positive thing for me right now, taxes or not."

"There it is!" she shouted, and turned the car sharply to the left. Sam squawked, and held on tighter.

The little car lurched upon two wheels for a moment, but somehow made the turn into a large opening in one of the tall buildings, bursting through the barrier without stopping to take ticket. The unseelie riders swerved about and shot into the open arch and up the ramp behind them.

Morgan hit the ramp and sped up it. The ramp was narrow, narrower than the street had been, and it only took a slight shimmy in the back end of the car to keep the unseelie sidhe from moving up to pace them and possibly do them harm.

Unfortunately, this situation would not last long. There were only a few more feet of ramp, a sharp turn at the top, and then they'd emerge into the more open space of the first level of the parking garage. Given the deserted nature of the downtown area at this time of night, it would not be surprising if there was plenty of room in a mostly empty level of the garage for their opponents to work with.

"Think, Morgan," her brain raced. "Given what I had to work with, the garage was the right choice, but now we're heading for problems. Think!"

And then they roared up past the top of the ramp, around the turn at the top, and into the wide open spaces, elven hunters immediately pulling up on either side of them and drawing weapons.

"The ramp to the next level" Morgan realized "if I can get on that, that'll buy us a little time and I might think of something else."

She looked across the open parking area, seeing the ramp at the far end. It was going to take some good driving to get there. Unfortunately she was all the driver they had, so she was going to have to learn fast. Her heart pounding in her chest, Morgan floored the car, and shot across the parking level, elves in hot pursuit.

She managed to make it to the next ramp without any further damage, although it was a close thing at points. And then she was on the ramp, and the unseelie sidhe had to drop back or be crushed against the support pillars as they passed.

"We're in the clear at the moment, but in a minute, we'll be out in the open again and back in trouble" she thought. "Come on brain- do your stuff! Improvise!"

And then they were turning, and on the second level, and the elves could get at them again.

Picking up speed, the unseelie hunters shot straight ahead, trying to get besides them. Morgan wasn't sure what to do, but she thought that being predictable was a great way to lose this race; so she tapped her brakes slightly, to slow herself and then, as the elves shot by her, swerved into their paths, causing them to veer outwards.

Two riders went down hard, motor cycles skidding on their sides, and Morgan floored it, speeding for the ramp to the third level. In the mirror, she saw the other two racing after her, and the downed sidhe pausing for a moment, stunned, before beginning to get up again.

Then they were on the ramp to the third level, and their pursuers were back behind them again.

Following her into the open space of the third level, the hunters became more cunning. They gave the car more leeway to maneuver, making themselves less vulnerable to Morgan's maneuvers as they sought to get alongside the car. Two of them paced her, while the other two shot outwards so they could come in from an angle.

Morgan floored it again, racing for the ramp to the fourth level. Sam sat up in the passenger seat, claws hooked in the upholstery, looking out over the window frame and serving as a spotter.

Suddenly Sam shouted "Heads up, Morgan!" and

dropped down on the seat of the car, and the sharp business end of a long horse lance came bursting through the glass of the passenger window, shooting across the front seat at the level of a human head.

Morgan tucked her head back vigorously, the lance just grazing her chin as it slid through and out the driver's side with a crash of tinkling glass.

Argh!

She kept driving forwards. The shaft of the lance pushed up against her throat. Hard.

Tucking her chin, she braked sharply, put the car in reverse and backed up as fast as she could, pulling the lance away from her throat. She twisted the wheel and spun the car to the right in reverse, snapping the lance off with an audible crash and sending splinters of the weapon raining throughout the car. The torque of the pressure on the lance forced the rider off his bike and he went down hard, sliding out of sight.

Morgan shifted into drive and drove quickly forwards, her lap full of fragments of lance and an elf sprawled on the concrete behind her.

"You ok, Sam?" she croaked.

"I'm ok," said Sam from where he crouched on the passenger seat with his front paws over his eyes

And then they were at the fourth ramp.

Up the ramp, round the turn and out again, elven riders in hot pursuit and a straight race across open space to the next ramp and the next brief interval from assault-

But not this time…

As they hit the ramp, there was heavy thump and a shriek. An arm reached in the shattered driver's side window as they sped up the ramp to the fifth level. An elf had timed things too closely, and his mount was swept away forcibly as they hit the ramp. He was clinging to the side of the car, shrieking as the iron of the car's body against his skin began to burn him

In shock, Morgan kept driving as the elf clawed at her throat, looking for any purchase to pull himself off the iron and into the more insulated part of the car.

Sam let go of the upholstery and leapt across the seat into Morgan's lap. He stretched up and began to strike with tooth and claw at the unseelie hand, opening wounds in the shining skin.

The elf shrieked and drew his hand back; and then there was another loud thump, and it was suddenly gone.

"Thanks, Sam." said Morgan.

"No problem, sweetness." said Sam casually strolling back across the rocking seat and resuming his seat.

Around the turn, out into the fifth level now and another race for the next ramp upwards. Across the level with elves in pursuit, and roaring up the ramp to the sixth level. The car made the turn at the top on two wheels but somehow stayed upright and one hunter also made it around the curve.

One didn't; and went flying off the edge of the garage.

For just a moment, Morgan could see the rider in her rearview mirror, bursting through the side of the sixth level of the parking garage, flying into space and then separating from his bike in midair as he began the long hard plummet to the concrete far below.

Now she was on the top level under an open sky.

There was only one last hunter on her tail-one final sidhe to deal with before they could escape and move on.

The roof was a maze of pillars, planters and other obstacles. The ramp was far off, and there was no straight route to it. She would to need to do well to survive.

Morgan drove furiously for the down ramp, weaving and turning, trying to elude the unseelie rider pacing her. He'd put on a burst of speed and moved ahead, wheeling to come in from the side. He dropped his lance into place and brought it lower, aiming at her tires. He was trying to cripple the car like a picador does a bull and make her vulnerable. He revved his engine, and then charged straight at them.

Morgan veered away to avoid being struck by the lance. She heard a lighter rap as opposed to a heavy impact as the elf shot by her. The rap sounded metallic, so he hadn't managed to hit the tires

The elf turned quickly and came back again, aiming somewhat higher. Morgan swerved, weaving through the obstacles of the level, speeding for the ramp which would block his pursuit temporarily. Beside her, she heard Sam moving, and then she felt him pushing under her right elbow.

"Get out of the way, Morgan." Sam said, head and forequarters in the back seat.

"Look, Sam" she snapped. "Driving for our lives here and need every bit of movement that I can get. Don't block my arms, my friend."

"Ooompk" said Sam in a muffled fashion, and stayed where he was, still moving under her arm and distracting her. .

The elf was coming rapidly at her once more, lance gleaming in the moonlight. She looked at the angle of the lance, waited until the last moment, and veered out of the way again.

This time, she heard a more solid hit, but the car was still moving, and that was what counted.

She could still feel Sam underneath her elbow, moving and surging; and it was getting annoying now.

"Can you just get out of there?" she asked harshly. "You're blocking my elbow and cramping my driving style."

"Ooph" said Sam once again; and she felt him backing out from under her elbow. It seemed to take him forever to get out of there, and something hard passed under her elbow and out of the back seat after him.

Morgan was curious about what he was doing, but she didn't have a free eye to look.

"What are you up to? Sam? Sam?" she asked.

"Never mind." said Sam. "Just get him on the right."

The elf was coming from the left side, but trusting her cat, Morgan changed this. Cornering sharply, she turned her car away from the ramp, surprising the sidhe, who was expecting something different. He shot by her, and turned; and now he was on her right side, as requested.

"Now, run for it, Morgan! Floor it!" shouted Sam, and she pressed her foot to the floor, accelerating rapidly as she wove her way through the obstacles and headed for the down ramp to the levels below.

The hunter was coming up fast on the right behind them, and she was worried about this. She'd have to slow to make the turn onto the ramp or she'd go right off the side like that other elf had, and this was not the way she wanted to end her evening.

"Sam," she said, in increasing alarm. "if you're going to do something, it'd better be soon…"

She felt Sam stand on his hind legs beside her.

"Oomph. Mmmmph," he said once more, and moved towards the passenger's side; and then there was a clatter and a crash as something went out that window.

There was a roar to the right behind them as the bike accelerated, and then a horrendous metallic shriek as something went terribly wrong.

The car pulled rapidly away. Morgan sped forward again, grateful for every break and breath of fresh air the universe would buy her.

She hit the top of the down ramp and took it on two wheels, but managed to stay on concrete and not take flight out the side of the garage. In the rearview mirror, she saw a scene of carnage with angry elf and bits of bike sliding vigorously in all directions across the top floor of the parking facility. There was a bigger bump, a crash and a shriek of mingled rage and pain.

Morgan took a deep breath and then another as she sped down the ramp into the bowels of the concrete building.

"So, Sam" she said casually, "what did you just do?"

"Oh… that." said Sam casually, reclining once more on the seat. "I just looked in the back for what things they had that might get in the way of an angry elf. Did you know that a long handled ice scraper is not a good thing for a motorcycle to drive over? It seems that it flips up, inserts itself between the spokes of the wheel and causes all kinds of mechanical mayhem."

Morgan bit her lip to keep from laughing, and then she let loose and laughed anyway. It was good to be alive and free and not being chased by the unseelie sidhe even if it was only for a minute or two.

On the seat beside her, Sam smiled.

"Now hurry on up, girlfriend," he said. "We've got a gate to catch before it closes again tonight and I'm sure this is not the last barrier we'll face on our way to it."

The car pulled out of the garage and onto the street again, once more on its way.

The Lands That Lie Between

Forty
Elsewhere

Down below on the sidewalk next to the parking garage, an unhappy elf crawled out from under the wreckage of his motorcycle. He snarled in pain, and shook his fist at the distant and uncaring moon above him. He could hear the sound of some of his fellows limping down the ramp out of the garage above.

In the distance, he saw the little car disappearing. Those two might have escaped himself and his hunting brothers, but the servants of the seelie court were not home free as of yet.

He pulled a horn of darkened bone from his belt and began to blow upon it. The sound echoed down the concrete canyons on the abandoned night time city...

The Lands That Lie Between

Forty-One
Morgan

Ten minutes later and a mile down the road, the car was pulled over with dented hood carefully propped up. Morgan bent over, peering at the engine for she knew not what.

"Guess that last hit was harder than I thought." said the cat, stretching up to join Morgan in looking under the hood.

A cloud of steam over the engine block and sad little puddles of fluids on the road beneath told a sorry tale of a little engine that had taken all that it could.

Morgan looked at Sam. Sam looked at Morgan.

"So...I guess that means we're walking again." said Sam.

Morgan sighed and went to get her stuff. She pulled her duffle bag out of the back and the bottle of water the healer had pressed upon her

"You might want to take what's left of that lance shaft, too." said Sam. "We've got a long ways to walk yet and you may want something to lean on."

"And if we run into any more evil enchanted things" he brightened "you can bop them with it."

Morgan looked at the long wooden shaft for a moment. It was one more thing to carry...but Sam was right. A walking stick might be handy, and, if it came to that, any weapon was better than no weapon at this point.

She grabbed a heavy work glove from the trunk, and used it to rub down the lance shaft, removing any splinters and cracked wood. Once the splinters were gone, she took the shaft and leaned on it, testing it against her weight.

It'd do. The lance seemed strong enough for practical use in the hike ahead. They still had a long way to go.

"And perhaps I *can* bop something with it." she thought, feeling slightly more cheerful at that point.

"Let's get a move on." said Sam. "We've got a gate to get to, and it'll be closing soon. Don't want to miss it."

Morgan sighed. She shouldered her bag, picked up her new unseelie walking staff /souvenir and began to walk down the darkened street, her cat frisking along at her side.

"Where are we going?" she asked Sam.

Sam stopped dead. He placed himself in a classic "cat–seated–with–tail–wrapped–around–his–paws" pose. He sniffed the air delicately. He cocked his head to one side at a precise angle and listened. He licked one paw, and held it up to test the exact direction of the gentle night time breeze that was blowing.

"We're going that way," he said and gestured elegantly in the direction they'd already been going.

He then stood up and started walking in that direction again.

Morgan sighed again, but she had to give him credit. You didn't often get to see such an elaborate exhibition of sarcasm.

She kept walking herself, and the two of them vanished down the road together, still gently bickering.

Forty-Two
Morgan

Much later, Morgan and Sam were finally entering the part of the city where the gate was currently open. As they approached city center, Morgan could see down from the hills into the center of town

When looking with her normal eye, the darkened city seemed sleeping and still, the same city as it was on every other night. When Morgan closed that eye and looked with her seeing eye, a very different picture was revealed...

The heart of the city was alive with noise and activity. The old king had died; the call had gone out; and the time allotted was almost gone now, so bearers of light had little time left to reach the court for the light they carried to be counted. There were many uncanny beings abroad tonight in the sleeping city...

Not all were light bearers either. Many sought the streets and alleys to benefit from the chances this night brought them. Whether agents of unseelie nobles sent to stop seelie light bearers, or more informal opportunistic scavengers and night terrors eagerly seizing an opportunity, the streets and alleyways were alive with unseelie hunters and assassins.

Those who bore the seelie light had a challenging task to reach the open gate alive and unharmed, a challenge that became more difficult as time passed and the deadline grew closer. Their ranks were being thinned down by the gauntlet of unseelie warriors, and dwindling time meant the seelie scions could no longer wait for a safer moment, but must take whatever chance they could now, or not arrive in time.

From the hill, Morgan saw unseelie archers lying in wait for travelers approaching the gate. She saw a small wyvern hissing, spreading its wings in a threat display in the face of a cluster of hunched and lumpy little men. She saw a herd of pale horses galloping wildly with heart breaking beauty through the darkened streets.

She shivered. She knew the two of them had to pass through that gauntlet if they were to reach the court in time and that scared her, but even though she was scared, she knew this was something that she had to do. All she'd gone through in life to bring her to this point had taught her that some things were worth taking risks for.

"The longer we wait, the worse it's going to be." she said, to Sam as he stood peering down into the center of the city.

He nodded somberly.

"We'd best get going then" he said.

He thought a minute. "And once we get past all of the chaos down there and through the gates, perhaps there will be snacks," he brightened.

"I'll just be glad to get someplace dry to sit down for five minutes." she replied as they moved off down the hill.

Forty-Three
Elsewhere

The hunters had barricaded a major street, blocking another route to the gate to the seelie court, and had broken the street lights as well to conceal their trap. Time was short now, and those who bore seelie energy could no longer wait for a better time to pass the gate safely. They must arrive in court soon, or lose their chance to have their precious cargo count in choosing the next ruler of the sidhe.

The unseelie had other plans. No seelie light would pass through the gate.

They heard the sounds of an engine approaching them, roaring through the silence of urban canyons. The hunters arranged themselves behind their massive bikes. Spears were gripped firmly in armored hands, and archers nocked their arrows. None would pass tonight.

The sound came closer, and the hunters grinned fiercely at each other. Soon they'd have the fun of taking down another seelie traveler.

In the dim star light, a cycle with a massive rider flashed into view a block away, coming fast. It sped towards them. The unseelie braced themselves for impact.

Just short of the barriers, the rider heaved up on the handlebars; and as the hunters watched in disbelief, the motorcycle left the ground.

Time seemed to slow for a moment as, impossibly, man and machine floated through the air over the barriers and above their heads.

And then the motorcycle landed with a massive crash and time returned to normal. The rider kept his balance and kept going as the hunters turned and tried to regroup. Arrows flew after him but missed as he faded into the darkness once more.

A derisive "beep, beep" of the bike horn drifted back from out of the darkness.

Forty-Four
Elsewhere

As the motorcycle disappeared in the distance, a small figure watched from the shelter under a car.

"Typical" sniffed the fox spirit, before picking her way from shadow to shadow past the disordered warriors and towards the gate.

The Lands That Lie Between

Forty-Five
Elsewhere

The merrow had been able to come a long way by water, swimming in underground streams and finding her way through reservoirs, but the final leg of the journey must unfortunately be made on dry land, and she found herself out of her element.

She had been able to go subtly for much of the way, but the time was running out now and the streets were crowded.

She took one chance crossing an open boulevard, and fate smiled on her. She was fortunate again to find refuge in the shelter of a delivery truck as a band of unseelie soldiers passed by.

And then, her luck ran out.

In the distance, she heard the howling, the note that sings of a new scent found. She knew that sound.

She began running, heedless of subtlety now that it no longer mattered. She ran with heart and strength and terror- and in the end it was still not enough.

The pack caught her, and brought her down.

The Lands That Lie Between

Forty-Six
Elsewhere

The unseelie warriors held their positions behind the barricades, listening to the sound of an engine roaring away in the distance. He had won past them, but not every traveler could do that trick and, now that they were prepared for it, no one else would pass that way.

The noises faded into the silence of the nighttime city. Time passed.

With the rising of the crescent moon, they heard a staccato sound, echoing off the surrounding buildings in the distance. Irregular at first, but gradually gaining a rhythm. The sound of distant hoof beats in the darkness.

They couldn't see what was coming, but they prepared to stop it.

The sounds of many hooves grew near to the trap, echoing in the depths of the concrete canyons. The hunters braced themselves, preparing for the battle to come.

The sounds stopped; and, when nothing happened, they peered into the unlit street before them. Coming out of the darkness, a silver figure stepped delicately into sight before them. A pale and shining stallion stood in the middle of the darkened street, pawing gently at the pavement and looking at them with deep, inquiring eyes.

Unseelie hands tensed on dark weapons...

The stallion eyed them all for a moment. Then his nostrils flared and he reared up onto his hind legs, bugling furiously and striking out in front of him in challenge. The vibration of the stallion's cry cut through unseelie heads like a diamond knife, and many of them involuntarily dropped their weapons to clutch at their ears.

The white stallion bugled again, curveting on his hinder legs and striking out at the air. He dropped to his four legs, and galloped in a tight, precise circle until he faced them once again.

And then, ears tight to his skull and eyes narrowed, he snorted, bared his teeth, and charged the line of sidhe ahead. The sound of many hoof beats echoed behind him.

For a single moment, the sidhe looked at each other in horror before the rest of the herd broke into view.

A tidal wave of mares was approaching them rapidly; mares of piebald, and brown, and black and white, sturdy foals running protected in the midst of the herd. Each one a solid mass of bone and hair and muscle, and together an unstoppable force of Nature. Ears back, teeth bared, foals squealing, hooves pounding, running with herd and hoof and heart, the herd ran, inexorably thundering towards them with the white stallion charging in the lead, bugling fiercely .

It was amazing. It was beautiful. It was terrifying. And it was coming their way...

The unseelie all gasped involuntarily at the beauty and the horror of the sight, and then the herd was upon them.

Spears half offered in defense were knocked aside and cracked like match sticks, barricades crumbled under the force of thousands of pounds of magnificent creatures, and the unseelie scattered to all sides to save their skins.

The stallion burst through the barriers first, and reaching the other side where the hunters were sheltering, turned on them in fury and lay about him, with massive teeth and muscle and four stout hooves striking out all around in turn. The remaining sidhe ran for their lives.

The stallion stood there, watching the hunters flee, chest heaving as the last of his people broke through the barriers in safety. His herd regrouped on the far side of the shattered jumps, forming up again in a safe and secure circle, mares outside and foals in the center, before passing him and thundering on in the direction of the gate to the elven court. A tiny speck of Light, held in each and every equine heart, shone faintly all around them and lit their path as they ran on towards the gate. The stallion pivoted, looking side to side to watch for unseelie stragglers before following his tribe once more into the darkness…

The Lands That Lie Between

Forty-Seven
Elsewhere

Wandering packs of predators roamed through the downtown area, looking for seelie sidhe or any other prey. The city was alive tonight.

A band of bogles passed down the street, clutching at each other with their strong clawed hands and chattering excitedly about what they would do to the next seelie creature they found.

They turned the corner and were gone again. Moments passed, and then the hob dropped down from the window alcove he had been hiding in. He moved on in a different direction, painfully alert for the next threat, but also thinking about the last few hours.

When the woman had distracted the hunters from him in the mall, he had taken the chance she had given him and gotten safely away. He could only hope that she had escaped as well. He knew if she hadn't saved him in the alleyway, and then again in the mall, he would not be alive now, and he was afraid she might have lost her life saving his.

He had started this journey with a responsibility to the court to bring his light to be weighed, but he now also owed that woman a debt and an obligation to use the life she'd given back to him wisely and well.

The city was full of danger tonight, and, as a small sidhe, it would be far safer for him to hole up until this entire thing was over with, but there are some debts that must be paid.

The hob braced himself and cautiously moved

onwards to his next hiding place.

Forty-Eight
Morgan

Time was running out for Sam and Morgan...

The summer king was gone, and the call out to all that carried the light within them to return to the court to have the measure of that light taken. A new ruler would soon be crowned, and the nature of that monarch chosen by the nature of the light returned.

It was important that a seelie ruler be crowned upon this day. The nature of the ruler determined the nature of the land, and they wanted it to be a land worth living in. An unseelie sidhe might find life difficult under a seelie king or queen, but a seelie sidhe living under unseelie rule was in a dangerous position.

The light must be returned to the court and weighed, and soon at that, and the way to the gate and from there to the court became more dangerous for those that bore the light with every moment.

Time was running out for Sam and Morgan...

Certain players on the unseelie side of court saw this as an ideal chance to control the lands that lay between and the mundane lands beside them by controlling how much seelie light returned to court. They were not fussy about how they did so, and sought to make the journey more difficult for those who carried the seelie light.

The streets and alleyways were alive with unseelie threats, not only hunters and assassins sent by unseelie nobles to make permanent arrangements for those that carried the seelie Light, but also more informal night terrors and opportunistic scavengers, who saw a good chance and were eagerly taking advantage of it. For the predators and scavengers, seelie meat was the sweetest and finest where they were concerned. Usually their prey took more care when going about their business.

Now the call was out to bearers of the light, and gave all the sidhe an undeniable urge to return to the court. Given the insistence of the call, and the obstacles of the unseelie, many seelie were distracted and did not take the precautions. This made some of them easy prey for an alert predator. It was not often that boggarts or red caps or darkhunds could so easily obtain the meat they desired above all others, and they were damned well going to take advantage of the situation.

Now it was true that not every seelie light bearer was as careless or vulnerable as they first appeared. Many an unseelie hunter set upon some distracted being or beast that seemed easy prey only to find out to their sorrow that they'd bitten off more than they could chew. Still, the ranks seelie light were thinned, and racing time meant the seelie scions could no longer wait for a safer moment, but must take what chance they could or not arrive in time.

Time was running out for Sam and Morgan…

Every nook and cranny, every alley and main street, every park and plaza in the downtown area had the potential to be an unseelie trap. The only questions were "Was there something in this space?", "What the heck is it?", "What's the best way around it?", and "Wouldn't it have been better to take a different route altogether?"

They'd hiked along back roads for hours after they'd left the crippled little car sitting sadly by the roadside. As they hiked, they watched for elven roadblocks, evaded unseelie patrols, and found their way through the silent midnight streets; but while they were hiking, the metaphorical clock was also ticking and the brief window before the open gate closed.

They had carefully stolen past several troops of roving hunters. They had avoided a pack of unseelie hounds hunting primarily by scent, by wading through an unappetizing culvert full of questionable liquid. They had vigorously swatted a swarm of vicious cannibalistic pixies. They had lost the lance fending off an aggressive bogey-beast. They had done all these and more besides by the time they hit the downtown area; but they knew it would only get more exciting from here. The closer they got to the gate and the time when the gate would close, the thicker the hazards and hunters lay upon the ground.

That time was remarkably close now...

Time was running out for Sam and Morgan...

They were running now, running from shadow to shadow, using what cover they could find to conceal them as they ran for the open gate.

Morgan slipped as she ran and went down hard on one knee, crying out with pain. The hunters heard her, and their chance of passing unnoticed was gone.

The unseelie smiled unpleasantly. They turned and

came running at her, weapons brandished high as they went. Sam dashed furiously at them, trying to block the elves and give her a chance to escape.

Morgan struggled to get to her feet, but her knee shrieked and buckled beneath her again. She fell heavily and rolled, trying to put less weight on the injured knee so she could stand and run.

One elf reached her, a massive figure with a broadsword clutched in his hand. He swung the sword overhead and brought it crashing down-only to have it stopped dead by a massive wooden staff that crossed in front of him at the last minute.

"That's no way to treat a lady," the tarot reader growled at him, before bringing the other end of the staff around for a crushing blow to the rib cage. Lifted off his feet by the force of the blow, the elf went skidding away with a little cry.

"Take my hand, dear" came a voice beside Morgan. "Let me help you." Suddenly, the palmist was at her side, helping her to her feet.

As Morgan leaned on the palmist's shoulder, she noticed for the first time how her ears were slightly pointed, and, when she closed one eye and looked through her seeing eye, she was surprised to see how much more light was shining around the two psychics.

The tarot reader quickly pivoted again, taking a protective stance between the women and the oncoming warriors, staff held across his body, ready to move rapidly as the need arose. Sam sprinted towards the little group of three.

"My dear" the palmist said to Morgan "I think its

best that we withdraw. Ah, and this must be your missing companion," said the palmist as Sam raced up to them. "Greetings to you, brother in fur."

Sam nodded briskly, to her and pivoted, beginning to weave to and fro between women and eleven warriors, a snare for the feet of any unseelie who got past the man.

The palmist sidled backwards steadily towards the gate, eyes scanning side to side as she went, keeping a careful eye out for incoming unseelie. Leaning heavily on the palmist's shoulder, Morgan limped roughly along with her, gritting her teeth against pain stabbing into her knee.

Her short, round supporter was keeping up a steady flow of chatter as she moved both of them towards safety. "This has certainly been a lovely bit of exercise we've had this evening, but I must say at this point I'll be just as glad to call it a day and go inside and have something nice to eat, won't you?" she asked Morgan.

Morgan nodded at her, teeth still gritted tightly against the pain; and the small part of her brain not already caught up in fear, pain or how the heck they were going to pull all of this off, noted the tarot reader and cat were backing slowly towards the gate as well, guided by the palmist's voice.

Pain forgotten for a second, Morgan looked at the palmist. Her companion winked briefly at her, and then continued backwards with a flood of foolish commentary as she helped Morgan towards the gate. Morgan's knee complained bitterly again, and all she could think of was pain and movement, step by labored step, that would move them out of danger and towards their goal.

The foursome slowly fought their way across the

open plaza towards the gate. A hunter lunged forwards and the tarot reader's staff swung around to block his weapon with an audible crack. Another thrust with a spear from the side, only to find his feet fouled by a passing cat. He fell heavily, spear flying from his hands.

"Excuse me" said the palmist, ducking away from Morgan. She darted forwards, avoiding swinging weapons, and scooped up the still rolling spear. She gave it a hard look and then returned to Morgan as quickly as she had gone.

"That'll do for the moment," she said, pressing the weapon into Morgan's hand. "Lean on this, and move as fast as you can to the gate. We'll cover you."

With that, the palmist stepped slightly forwards again, placing herself between Morgan and the unseelie, inside of the circle of protection already outlined by cat and tarot reader.

"Best get a move on, gentlemen" she said loudly. "We've an important appointment to keep and the powers that be do not like to be kept waiting."

Removing her purse from her shoulder and holding it dangling from both hands, she resumed chattering to guide reader and cat as she backed once more towards the gate, part of the shield between Morgan and sidhe.

As they all sidled towards the gate, their attackers became more aggressive. Soon there were warriors lunging in from both sides, trying to break through their defenses. The tarot reader's staff swung widely through the air, clearing hunters from one side, sharply reversing to catch a stray sidhe who'd thought he'd seen an opening. Sam sprang into the air, clawing the face of another hunter in mid–flight. Yet another predator cut in on the flank, diving behind cat and tarot reader, only to be struck hard and stunned by the palmist's bag.

Morgan knew her injury was slowing them, keeping them in danger. She leaned on the spear and hobbled towards the gate as fast as she could.

One on one, they were doing well in protecting themselves and watching out for each other; but there were more predators at this point than they could handle, and the sound of the combat was attracting others to the area. It was important to get themselves through the gate before time ran out.

Morgan reached the gate first. She'd passed this place a number of times and never seen any gate before. Now two buildings that normally abutted on each other somehow seemed to have slid several feet apart, revealing a shining gateway faced in white marble gleaming like moonbeams. The street was softly illuminated by the glow of the gate, casting a magickal radiance over a mundane midnight street. Morgan hesitated at the very edge of the open gate, looking back at her companions and wondering if she should go through before them.

The gate was intimidating. She'd heard stories of people who went into the lands of faerie, never to return. If she passed through the gate, would she be able to come back to the world she knew if she wished? Would she be abandoning the palmist, tarot reader and Sam? For that matter, would she be safe once she passed through the gates, or would the unseelie only pursue her through the gate and into the unknown world beyond?

As she stood there wavering and watching her

companions, a small red fox came flowing like velvet up to the gate at her feet. Morgan recoiled, unsure whether this small creature was friendly or another source of danger.

The small fox paused there on the threshold of the gate, tipping its sharp head up to look at her with deep and knowing eyes. "Girl" said the fox "what are you waiting for? Is not this what you have come through danger and magick and mystery for?" With a pert flick of her auburn tail, the fox was over the threshold, through the open gate and gone from the lands of Man.

Morgan blinked twice. All at once, her concerns felt foolish. The fox was right

She looked once more at her fellows. They were closer now and would soon reach her. She'd have to choose soon anyway-so, why not now?

Morgan gripped her spear firmly and took a deep breath. Just before the combat reached her, she stepped resolutely through the gate.

Forty-Nine
Morgan

There was gentle tingling along her skin and a subtle change in the air as Morgan stepped through the gate. It reminded her of going into an air conditioned house when the air outside was thick and hot and humid.

The walls were tall and stately, made of pale white marble that shone with subtle light. A sheltered guard's station stood on each side of the gate, but no guards were visible. The halls stretched out ahead as far as she could see. As she passed through the gate, Morgan looked up and saw the tips of a metal portcullis high in the open space above the gateway. It was clear she was in a different world from the one she'd come from.

Far ahead, she saw the proud tail of the fox, floating delicately along the hall and making good time despite precise and stylish movement. She heard the sound of hoof beats somewhere beyond her sight. There were hints of other movement further in the distance.

"Not much time left." thought Morgan, turning to look for her companions. "We'd better move fast, or we'll be too late."

Looking back through the gate with both eyes was like watching something on an old TV. The view was fuzzy to the eye, the colors muted, and the world she saw beyond the gate seemed slightly unreal when viewed from where she stood.

Things changed, however, when she closed one eye and looked through her seeing eye alone. A sheen of flowing light marked the boundary between elven worlds and lands of man, a curtain of light shimmering with a thousand different colors. It was so uncanny and beautiful that the breath caught in Morgan's lungs, and she took a single step backwards.

Stepping back, she finally saw into the guards' stations…

Two figures, slumped down on the floor and curled up tight upon themselves, carefully hidden. Two pools of blood, fluid on marble floors and spreading around each huddled figure. Two deep silences, of two beings long gone beyond halls of elves and men.

Morgan's eyes opened wide. She opened her mouth wide too, and screamed aloud. "It's a trap!" she shrieked, lunging towards the gate. "The guards are dead!"

Beyond the gate, her companions were hard pressed by the gathering warriors, increasing by the moment. The psychic's staff flashed fiercely about him, and Sam was everywhere at once, tricking, tripping, distracting, attacking.

The palmist threw a quick look over her shoulder at Morgan. "It may be a trap" she shouted, swinging her heavy bag again and felling another predator "but right now, it's the best option we've got."

She continued to back towards the gate.

Morgan knew there must be a way to close the gate once her friends had entered. Looking frantically around, her eyes saw the chain stretching down from portcullis to winch but the mechanism was locked beyond hope of repair by a javelin jammed deep in its gears.

"Fall back!" she heard the palm reader shouting. "Fall back to the gate! We're almost out of time!"

Morgan moved to just inside of the gate, leaning against the outside of the box to free her hands to use her spear. She watched the tarot reader use his staff to defend and attack as her companions edged closer. That'd be her job soon enough-she'd best pay attention while she could. As she watched, the light in the gate flickered and faded and the world outside became less distinct.

"Hurry!" she screamed. "The gate is closing!"

Outside the gate, cat and psychics backed up faster, but the unseelie also pressed them harder. They could only move so fast without leaving themselves open to attack. Once, and once, and yet once again, Morgan saw an elven weapon come perilously close to one of them, only to be blocked or parried at the last minute by one of the others...

The light was fading faster now, and the outside world becoming more and more indistinct; fading away in Morgan's sight. "Hurry up!" she cried loudly again. "You're almost out of time!"

The palmist reached the gate first, glancing quickly over her shoulder to keep herself on course and chattering like a human GPS for the others. She backed neatly through the gate, and pivoted into position, back pressed against the sentry wall directly opposite Morgan. Her bulky bag was still held ready as an improvised flail.

Their eyes met across the opening. In a flash of inspiration, Morgan reached back into the sentry box and, with effort, snapped off the javelin shaft.

"Heads up!" she cried out to her counterpart, and tossed it across the gap to the palmist. The woman gaped at her for an instant, but caught the stick neatly out of the air while continuing to shout directions to cat and psychic still fighting outside the gate. The palmist slung her heavy bag back over her shoulder, and then rotated the shaft to use as an improvised staff. Both women turned as one towards the gate to watch their companions edge towards the relative safety of the elven halls.

The light in the gateway continued to fade.

The area before the gate had become a bottleneck, with predators both great and small drawn to it as if by some metaphysical magnet. In a way, this almost helped the pair, as darkling forces were packed so close that they got in each other's way. Many an unseelie warrior had his sword fouled by his fellows, and many a darkling beast trampled into the ground under the paws of another eager for the coming feast. There was a great deal of unseelie cursing in a variety of tongues.

While many of their foes were doing more damage to each other, many blows were being thrown, and some were getting through. The tarot reader bled from a dozen small cuts on hands and legs. Sam just avoided having his tail fashionably bobbed. There were too many sidhe for the pair to beat them all.

Man and cat reached the gate at last.

The colors in the gate swirled wildly as the tarot reader backed through them. He moved rapidly deeper into the hall before taking a centered stance, preparing for a renewed attack. The cat leaped through a moment later, turning gracefully in midair to face the open gate as well. A low wail rumbled deep in his throat as he backed down the hall. Against the sentry boxes, the women braced themselves and edged down the walls toward their companions, eyes fixed on the gate.

There was a moment's pause. The colors swirled more madly than before. Then, with a wild and savage cry, the unseelie forces poured through the gate like a river in flood.

Morgan and the palmist backed quickly down the walls to join their fellows. Cat and the tarot reader spread out to meet the women and give themselves room to defend themselves. Unseelie predators continued to rush in through open gate and the swirling light. Swords flashing. Fierce growling. A wave of unseelie warriors and uncanny beasts.

Then, with a roar and a flash and a final shriek, the flowing light blazed once brightly.

And went out.

The gate slapped forcibly shut.

Some predators, neither in nor out when the gate closed, were caught in between one world and the next. This was not a good thing for them. Morgan thought wildly that, as little as three days ago, she would have cried out in horror, turned quickly away, or possibly even thrown up at the sight before her; but now she was too busy staying alive to react.

"What a difference a couple of days makes" she thought hysterically as she smote and limped and backed her way down the hall.

Her companions were busy too as they were still attacked from all sides, but, bit by bit, they were making gradual progress down the hall, and bit by bit, there were fewer and fewer sidhe attacking them, as their little group took their toll. Crack! A staff took an unseelie sidhe across the ribs and sent him flying. Snarl! A beast recoiled with a savagely clawed muzzle. Crash! And another warrior went flying, tripping over a deftly inserted stick.

The little group continued to make progress towards their time sensitive goal.

"Pick up the pace!" shouted the palmist. "It's not enough to pass the gate before it closes. If we don't reach the central court in time, our light won't count and this will all have been wasted."

"Then let's make time then!" roared the tarot reader smiting another opponent with his oaken staff. He sped up, forcing the others to do likewise. As more and more adversaries fell back bloody or bruised, moving became easier. They were still beset but no longer spent every moment to fending off death. They moved faster.

The endless halls flew by, and they came to a turn. They were still attacked but the pace was easier and they seemed home free. Rounding the corner, they were racing, heels clattering against marble, breath pounding in their lungs, and sticks lashing out to keep pursuers at bay. At the end of the hall, they saw an open doorway with a light shining through it.

"There it is!" shouted the palmist. "The central court! We're almost there!"

They passed one doorway, and then a second. As they passed the third, an immense figure stepped out of the shadows and reached out with an impossibly long arm, snagging Morgan around the neck, pulling her out of the group.

"Ack!" Morgan said, as her air was cut off...

And everything stopped dead.

Cat, palmist and tarot reader formed a protective circle in the middle of the hall, back to back, watching encircling hunters as well as Morgan and her captor. The unseelie prowled the outside of the circle, growling and threatening.

A dark and deep voice sounded from somewhere above Morgan's head.

"So it seems we're at something of an impasse…" the voice said pleasantly yet ominously "I'm not seeing this ending in any way that everyone will like."

Morgan stood very, very still. A muscular arm was tight around her throat, jerking up until she had to stand on her toes to keep breathing. She was afraid she might pass out, but she knew she couldn't afford to. It was only by standing as upright as she was that she was getting any air at all. Pass out and she'd have her air cut off and suffocate, if this fellow didn't snap her neck first. She had no illusions that he cared about her well being. He'd as soon kill her as not. She'd seen how the unseelie were dealing with the carriers of the seelie light, and was not minded to be part of any unseelie solution.

"As I see it" the voice continued. "I've something that you want; and you've something I want. We'll all do better if we start by agreeing on that."

Morgan saw through watering eyes that the tarot reader was looking fiercely at the voice above her head. The palmist reader nodded once.

"Your point being…" she said.

"Now you want this precious little bundle here" said the dark voice. "And I do not necessarily have a need for her. But, if I broke her neck, you'd not have her either…"

He gave Morgan a shake for emphasis.

"He's right." thought Morgan. "I don't see this

going anywhere I'd like; but the good part is that, right now, he's not paying any attention to me."

She began to slide her hand downwards towards the purse clasped around her waist.

"Now, I would prefer that there no longer be a seelie ruler of the elven court" the voice above her head continued. "A change of administration would be to my advantage; and if you arrive in court and make your contribution, this is far less likely."

"I'm listening.... " said the palmist, her face set.

Morgan's hand quietly unzipped her purse, sound masked by ominous conversation.

"The easiest way to resolve this would be to snap this pretty little neck" the voice said darkly "and then address my issues directly with the rest of you; but it will certainly be good enough to stand here and let the time elapse. Since I'm kind and equitable, I think we'll just wait for time to run out."

The tarot reader raised his staff slightly. The grip tightened on Morgan's throat.

"Oh no" said the voice quietly "you do not want to put me in a position when I have to do anything... final..."

And Morgan reached into her purse and, firmly grasping a nail, pulled it out in a rush and jabbed it into the arm that held her up to its cold iron head.

There was a shriek from above her, a cry of anguish. The arm tightened unbearably, but Morgan reached up and pulled down on it with all of her strength, turning her face into the elbow to get some breathing space. That bought her enough time for the tarot reader to charge and pull her away from her unseen captor.

She stood in the middle of the hall gasping for breath and rubbing her bruised throat, while cat and palmist and tarot reader surrounded her, weapons ready. Unseelie beings circled round, looking for an opening.

A voice rang out from the open door beyond…

The Lands That Lie Between

Fifty
Morgan

...A voice rang out from the open door beyond.

"Hold!" it thundered. "Hold thy weapons! All doth know that there shall be no fighting in the court while the new king is being chosen!"

Morgan shot a look at the doorway. A large sidhe stood there, ornate staff brandished in one hand.

"Sam," she muttered out of the side of her mouth. "The door. It's full of elf."

"That's the steward of the court." the cat purred back. "Now we'll see something."

"All combat is forbidden in these halls until the new king is decided." the steward roared "and the enchantments in this place have given me the power to see that this is accomplished. Let each of thee put up thy weapons then; lest, for thee, there be ...consequences..."

The tarot reader immediately dropped his staff into a "ready" stance, and the palmist lowered the javelin. Sam deliberately sat and began casually washing one paw.

The unseelie majority were slower to react. Most unwillingly drew back, but one hunter raised his axe and, with a cry, leapt towards the psychics.

The steward moved his staff slightly. There was a burst of light, and the hunter was gone, as if he had never been.

"Consequences." the steward emphasized as he turned back into the central court. Hordes of armed soldiers poured out of the doorway and surrounded the combatants, escorting them into the court behind the steward.

The court room beyond the door was vast, in keeping with the corridors that lead to it. Marble pillars stretched upwards to a distant roof. Decorative friezes lined the walls. Lush carpets covered the floors, easing the echoes of the massive space.

The steward strode down a wide aisle leading to the front of the court.

A mass of beings filled the spaces on either side of the aisle. Elves, yes, but humans too, and other persons, as well as those who went on four legs or on wings, and not only seelie folk either. Here a boggart, shifted between one form and another. There a dark horse with red eyes pawed the ground and bared pointed teeth. Not every being was a light bearer. Many, like Sam, had come accompanying one, or to bear witness to the future of the Lands Between, but there were many who bore the light within them and were there to be counted.

Morgan walked carefully down the aisle, watchful amongst this uneasy truce. Ahead of her, the procession slowed as it came closer to the front of the hall. Those who carried light remained in line to be counted, and their companions turned off into the crowds on the sides.

Morgan saw the palmist stop three places in front of her, and herself stopped in turn. Standing, she noticed an unseelie band in front of her to the side. One warrior seemed particularly tense, his hand on the hilt of his sheathed sword.

Consequences or not, the sight of him made her nervous. She moved over, so she'd be on the far side of the line from him.

At the front of the aisle was a raised dais with a

throne at the top. The throne upon that eminence was empty now, speaking volumes. Below, the steward stood before the assembled multitude beside a massive scale. Hanging from each arm of the scale was a large stone urn. One was of alabaster pale and bright and the other was of jet as dark as any midnight. Both urns shone luminously from within.

By the look of the scale, the count was close.

The steward gestured, and a tall pale woman stepped forwards, shining brightly. The steward raised his staff of office, and the brightness rose out of her to shine in the air above the crowd for a moment, before descending into the alabaster urn.

The balance of the scale shifted slightly, the alabaster urn descending.

The steward gestured again. The woman stepped aside and the dark horse stepped forwards. The steward's staff rose again, and the light rose out of the horse and flowed into the urn of jet.

The balance shifted once again.

One by one, each one moved forwards and took its place for its light to be collected and measured in the choosing of the new king.

Ahead of her, the palmist reached the front. The light she carried rose and was drawn into the alabaster urn. Despite this, the jet urn still weighed heavier in the scales.

The palmist turned aside and took her place in the crowd, husband and cat working their way up to join her. The next being was weighed and the next after that, and then it was Morgan's turn.

She stepped into place and the steward raised his

staff once more. Light flowed out of her, out of her eyes, her mouth, her heart, her skin, flowing out and up into the aether, leaving her feeling lightheaded.

The light hovered for a moment above her head before descending into the alabaster jar. The urn glowed more brightly and then subsided. Feeling dizzy and a bit empty, Morgan moved to the side, joining her friends.

The scale rebalanced.

Only a double handful of beings were yet to be counted and, by looking at the balance, Morgan could see the measure would be close. She huddled tightly with her friends, watching anxiously as the scale tipped slightly to one side and then the other as the last few light bearers were counted.

The last one stepped to the front. It was unseelie, and Morgan's heart sank just looking at it.

The steward's rod of office rose, the light drifted upwards, and then dropped into the urn of jet.

The scale shifted- and the jet urn was slightly but clearly heavier. The new king would be unseelie, and cruelty would be loose in the lands. Morgan turned and buried her face in the palmist's shoulder to hide her tears. The tarot reader wrapped his arms around them both, and Sam rubbed against her leg.

Unpleasant cheers and jeers and threats were already arising from various beings in the court. The steward, face stricken, bent down to carefully check the scales and the balance to be sure of an accurate response. That done, he rose and opened his mouth to officially announce the results to all there assembled.

"Excuse me." said a voice from the distant

doorway. "Excuse me. Am I too late?"

The entire court turned in surprise. There, in the door, a small figure was standing. A hob.

Morgan's eyes widened with recognition.

"No" said the steward, startled but suddenly hopeful. "No thou art not. Come forward and be weighed."

The hob walked forward, and heads turned to follow as he passed. He seemed uncomfortable with all of the attention, but he continued to walk, reaching the front of the court room at last.

He stood, dwarfed by his surroundings, as the steward gestured with his rod of office. A great light rose out of him and shone above the crowd before descending into the alabaster urn.

The scale tipped one final time.

"The Lands that Lie Between shall have a seelie king!" the steward proclaimed, voice echoing through the marble halls. Cheers rang out, but noticeably not from all the beings in the hall.

Morgan's eyes shot to the right. She saw the dark warrior she had been watching begin to draw his sword. She tensed.

And then another unseelie sidhe put a cautionary hand on the hilt, stopping the sword in mid draw. When the first sidhe looked up in surprise, the new one gave him a fierce look, and slightly shook his head.

The first one tensed, and then let his blade slide back into its' sheathe again.

Morgan eased slightly. Trouble, yes-there would be trouble.

But not today.

The Lands That Lie Between

She joined the cheering.

Fifty-One
Morgan

It was two weeks later, and Morgan was sitting at a table on the outside patio of the tea shop with a duffle bag at her feet. "You've really got to find some more cat friendly places to get together with your friends" the duffle said.

"Hush" she said, nudging the bag with her toe. "This place brings back fond memories."

"Of all of two weeks ago" said the bag sulkily.

The back door opened, and palmist and tarot reader emerged, hands filled with cardboard trays full of goodies. They crossed to her table, settled themselves and began passing out food and drink.

"Leave some room at the end" said Morgan. "We've got one more coming- and here he is now" she said, as the back door opened again. The biker shambled across the patio and pulled up a wrought iron chair.

Food and drink distributed, they all dug in with a will, and there was silence, broken only by the sound of chewing, yummy noises and a duffel bag wheedling.

"So, am I supposed to call you "Your Majesty" now?" Morgan asked the biker teasingly.

He grinned back at her. "Well, on formal occasions, it would probably be a good idea, but for times like these, not unless you feel like it." he said.

He ran his hand distractedly through his hair, standing it on end. "It's a lot to take on, but someone has to do the job. The exciting part will be explaining all of this to my lady. It was one thing when it was just a small part of my life, but I think she's going to notice when official messengers start showing up."

They laughed. "She doesn't know?" the palmist said.

"Not yet" said the biker. "Up to now, it wasn't important, but things have changed. Fortunately, I was lucky enough to find someone who's smart and adaptable, and luckier still that she seems like she loves me too. If I make a go of being king, it'll be because I've got her help."

"So I'd better tell her soon" he said with a wry face. I've just got to figure out how."

A ginger head popped out of the top of the duffle. "You could start her out easy" said Sam. "You could take me home for dinner and introduce her to a talking cat."

"Sam, the first time you talked to me, I fainted" said Morgan. "Are you sure that's starting her easy?"

"You only fainted because you got hit with too much at once." said the cat earnestly. "By myself, I'm very loveable."

The biker smiled. "I'll think on that and get back to you. How are you doing?" he said, turning to Morgan. "Recovered yet from your adventures in the faerie lands?"

"Getting there" she said. "But it's a lot to process."

"You were touched by faerie before" said the tarot reader "but now you have been over the borders and seen what lies there. They say that, once you visit the land of the faerie, you can never truly return to the lands of man."

They were all silent for a moment.

"Don't be silly, love" said his wife, poking his arm and breaking the mood. "You can go back and forth as often as you like. You've just got to know when and where the gates are."

"When and where the gates are!" gasped Morgan. "That reminds me! I've got an overdue library book! Excuse me, folks."

And, grabbing duffle in one hand and sandwich in the other, she was gone.

The other three sat there blinking for a moment.

"Funny girl" the tarot reader finally said. "but I'm sure we'll be seeing her again."

"Good" said the palmist. "The world needs more heroes. Both worlds do. My, this curried chicken sandwich is good…"

And they sat and ate and talked until the sun went down again.

The Lands That Lie Between

Glossary

Aura- energy field surrounding a living being.

Boggart- a malicious goblin.

Brownie- Small sidhe who makes himself responsible for for the place where he lives and comes out at night to do tasks not completed.

Darkhund- Large unseelie hound.

Energy worker- One who affects the physical world through non-physical means such as spells or intent.

Faery/Fae- Other names for elves or fairies.

Glamour- An illusion often used by the fae. Used to make people see what the caster wants, and, in extreme cases, do what the caster says.

Hag- One type of female sidhe, ugly and aggressive.

Hearth Spirit- protective spirit of a home

Hob- Kindly, beneficent and occasionally mischievious spirits

The Lands that Lie Between- the lands of the faerie world that lie side by side with the human world like the pages in a book.

Merrow- The Irish equivalent of a mermaid.

Rade- A ride or procession of trooping fairies. Dangerous to approach.

Red cap- One of the most malignant goblins. Named for his red cap, which he dies in the blood of his victims.

Seelie- Name given to the more kindly elven court. Seelie sidhe can be dangerous, but not intentionally cruel.

Sidhe- Another name for elves, as well as for other related magickal creatures.

Unseelie- The more malevolent elven court, never under any circumstances favorable to mankind.

Warding- Method of energetically protecting a place from malevolent beings or energies.

Wards-Tools used for warding a place

Catherine Kane is a teller of tales, a poet, wordsmith and songwright, an artist, an enthusiastic student of the Universe, a maker of very bad puns, and a medieval re-enactor who spends a lot of time at renaissance faires, when she isn't hunched over her netbook writing.

She is also a bit of an over achiever.

Want to keep in touch with what she's up to? Find her at http://catherinekanewrites.wordpress.com/ and on Facebook at https://www.facebook.com/pages/Catherine-Kane-Writes/134304556668759

www.ingramcontent.com/pod-product-compliance
Lightning Source LLC
Chambersburg PA
CBHW031144050726
47495CB00018B/989